INVASION OF THE LUST KITTENS

I had no idea there was a subway station in McGulveyland. One expects magic places to be unspoiled, bucolic. But down here everything is chrome and glass.

A train goes through, and in one of the windows I catch a glimpse, for less than a second, of a naked woman with cat whiskers.

So the worst has happened. The lust kittens— time witches—have broken out of the book I brought into Mr. McGulvey's magic library, and are now spreading their anarchy everywhere. . . .

In
Between
Dragons

MICHAEL KANDEL

BANTAM BOOKS
NEW YORK • TORONTO • LONDON • SYDNEY • AUCKLAND

IN BETWEEN DRAGONS

A Bantam Spectra Book / September 1990

ISBN 0-553-28814-8

Published simultaneously in the United States and Canada

Bantam Books are published by Bantam Books, a division of Bantam Doubleday Dell Publishing Group, Inc. Its trademark, consisting of the words ''Bantam Books'' and the portrayal of a rooster, is Registered in U.S. Patent and Trademark Office and in other countries. Marca Registrada. Bantam Books, 666 Fifth Avenue, New York, New York 10103.

PRINTED IN THE UNITED STATES OF AMERICA

RAD   0 9 8 7 6 5 4 3 2 1

Chapter One

• 1 •

Rest and recreation in McGulveyland, after battling the dragons of Cuspidor for a month straight. My breath still comes out pale green and stinking of vinegar. The lesions are healing nicely here, thanks to the poultices of V. Snerk and, of course, the climate. The air in McGulveyland heals everything. Sometimes I ask myself: Sherm, why don't you spend *all* your time in McGulveyland? Why knock yourself out on these stupid adventures? What do they get you?

They never turn out the way you expect. They twist. They're booby-trapped, like the contract Phineas P. Doubleday signs in blood in order to get a million bucks, have Miss September in bed with him, and live two hundred years. Ha-ha-ha, goes the hollow, echoing, diabolical laughter on the last page. You sap!

I have the sneaking feeling sometimes that it's all part of my educaton. That it's really Mr. McGulvey giving me growing-up lessons while I'm just trying to have some fun. I'm sure he has the power to pull strings like that behind the scenes. They're his books, after all. Not that he'd ever admit it. No, Mr. McGulvey is indirect, like a Zen master. He wouldn't come out and lecture you if his life depended on it. But steering, in his own silent, hands-off way? Yes, that's possible.

From Mr. McGulvey, somehow, I don't mind. It's not like Mom.

2

They gave me my armor first thing when I arrived in Cuspidor. It wasn't your ordinary armor—steel, brass, and chain mail—but all high-tech, lightweight. Teflon, ceramics, treated polymers. Sir Frank explained:

"Against the chemicals the dragons use, traditional materials are useless. We had a guy here last month who insisted on a Camelot suit. After a day it was so badly corroded, we had to use an acetylene torch to get him out."

"Without burning him?" I asked.

Sir Frank squinted at me, as if I had said something unbelievably half-witted. "Of *course* it burned him. What do you think?"

From this I saw that these knights were tough. And, if they were tough, that meant they had to be tough. The situation, in other words, was serious. It was war in this adventure, not a polite afternoon of parry-and-thrust between tea and biscuits. I set my jaw.

As soon as I was outfitted, I took a look at the town, because it's always a good idea to familiarize yourself beforehand with the terrain. In the heat of the moment it can save your life to remember that around the corner is a grove of trees or a drugstore to duck into.

Cuspidor was actually a full scale city; it had bridges, high office buildings all in glass and geometric aluminum, and there was even a slum. I went on foot, pretending to be just another pedestrian, and checked things off in my head. A subway system. Parks. Traffic. Statues commemorating founding fathers.

The reservoir north of the city told the story. The water was Popsicle green, with evil purple blotches floating here and there; bubbles rose steadily from the depths and gave off gray and yellow gases. When the wind changed, I got the full smell, and was almost knocked over. Lemon feces.

Then, overhead, high up, against a cloud, I caught a glimpse of the enemy. Tail, fangs, bat wings. I couldn't see much detail at that distance, but the thing looked smug.

So the dragons had the upper hand, were probably winning. How was I going to turn the tables?

The official at the Department of Health confirmed my fears. He riffled the papers on his desk and sighed. "Yes, Sir Sherm," he said, unable to look me in the eye, as if somehow he was to blame. Though, really, what could a civil servant be expected to do against mythological monsters? "The mortality rate in the last year has rocketed. Cancer of the liver, one out of ten people, an epidemic, and getting worse."

At this rate the whole city would be a graveyard in a couple of months, and what wasn't a graveyard would be hospitals full of freaks, tumors growing out of their ears and foreheads, etc.—and we were talking about millions of people. Men, women, and innocent children. "Something has to be done," I said, clutching the hilt of my sword in anger.

An unpleasant twist to this adventure came when I was taken to my "steed." It was no horse stable Sir Frank led me to after all the briefing, it was a parking lot. My charger was a 1966 Dodge Dart, six-cylinder, two-door, tan, with a rust problem. The upholstery was a mess, in shreds.

"This'll be yours," said Sir Frank, handing me the keys apologetically.

I blushed. Not because it was an affront to my knightly dignity or a disappointment—but let Sir Frank think that. The fact was, I didn't know how to drive. We'd only had two weeks of driver's ed at Whitney, and Mr. Bromberg was awful. All he did was mumble, mumble. I hadn't even got behind the wheel. Just quizzes, a lot of stupid questions about carburetors, spark plugs, and how many feet to stop from a school bus. So this really put me on the spot.

Scowling, as if indignant, I peered in, praying for the car at least to be automatic. No such luck: a stick shift. Could I fake driving? I doubted it. The pedal to the right—was that the clutch or the brake? Sick to my stomach, palms sweating, I came close to throwing in the towel, phasing back to McGulveyland, and to hell with the doomed populace of Cuspidor. After all, they were only characters in a book.

Except that Mr. McGulvey, if he happened to look in that particular volume on the shelf of his library, would see Sherm pop in and pop out of the adventure almost on the same page, with coward written all over his adolescent face. It would be right there in black and white, documented. So I said to myself: Sherm, baby, hang in for a while more. You can phase out anytime.

(I didn't know my hand signals, either. Damn, damn.)

The knights were quartered in what resembled a firehouse. There was even a pole to slide down when the siren went off. Sir Frank introduced me around, and I shook hands. There was, first, Sir Bob, who looked a lot like Dan Aykroyd. Then Sir Phil, incredibly fat for a knight, with a belly that constantly got in his way and a puffy lower lip that made his words come out babyish. Then Sir Josh: modest, quiet, a master swordsman. Sir Gawain, no relation to the famous Sir Gawain, King Arthur's nephew, but an easygoing guy who loved pizza. Sir

Mike, scientifically minded and into bodybuilding (he hurt my hand). And Sir Gardyloo, whom I knew from a previous adventure. Sir Gardyloo and I had been in a dungeon together for a whole week on the planet Saraband, and between us the body odor got unbelievably rank, since the dungeon was smaller even than my bedroom and there were no showers. We were freed by Princess Martha Anne disguised as a monk. But I digress.

The eight of us formed a company. There were other companies of knights in Cuspidor, stationed in other firehouses, but we rarely socialized with them. There wasn't time, with all the action. And most were quickly killed. The men whose hands I shook that sunny afternoon, on the day of my arrival, would all be dead, fallen in battle, within the week.

3

Sherman had to walk Terhune. Sighing, he got the leash. In the old days, the dog jumped up and did a wiggling dance of joy, tail swishing, at the sound of the choke chain slipped from the peg in the closet. But Terhune was almost twelve now, ancient, his coat dull, his eyes filmy and half-blind, his legs weak, and his body fat and full of lumps. He smelled like a rag forgotten under a basement sink. Sherman wished the dog would die and get it over with. In the old days, as boy and dog, they had been best friends, chasing each other in windy fields, and Terhune's barking had been almost like human laughter, like shouts in a playground or from a pool packed with kids in the middle of July. The thing to do was call the dog people, the pound, and have them put Terhune to sleep. Into the truck with him, turn on the carbon monoxide.

Let Priscilla the Pill drop big tears if she wanted—she was always glad for an excuse to produce those baseball-size tears. She never really cared about the dog. (Girls didn't care about dogs, only cats.) Sherman entertained, for a moment, the criminal thought: Maybe the SPCA men would put Priscilla the Pill, too, in the truck. Then he could say, "Gosh, Mom, sorry. They must have mistaken her for a stray mutt." Sherman put on his jacket and took Terhune out, to the lot. Not to the creek, where there were bushes, trees, and the illusion, if you looked in the right direction, that you were in the country. The creek was too far now for the old dog, eight blocks, and Sherman, anyway, wanted to get the walk over with as soon as possible. The lot was ugly. There was litter—people dumped their trash there, lawn cuttings that rotted—but mainly it was where everyone in the neighborhood took his dog to squat. Sometimes you could see three or four people in a row, holding their leashes, and at the end of each leash a dog, maybe big, maybe little, squatting. If you left the sidewalk, you had to pick your way carefully between turds of all kinds: reddish, blackish, whitish, some dried out, some still wet and steamy brown, and the occasional sickening puddle of doggy diarrhea, lemon yellow. Sherman closed his nose and breathed through his mouth as he led Terhune into the lot. The old dog sniffed around halfheartedly and slowly prepared himself for the effort of squatting. Sherman looked the other way.

4

Mr. McGulvey looks up at me. He's been examining a butterfly collection through a magnifying glass. His face is unshaven; a black-and-gray stubble covers his cheeks and chin. In the corner of his mouth is half a cigar, unlit. It gives off a strong, deep smell that reminds me of an old, extremely comfortable, cracked-leather armchair.

"Yes?" he asks, squinting politely.

I explain that I was drawn to this wonderful purple-heather mountaintop by the view, the vistas to all points of the compass, and happened to see, at the top of yon picturesque precipice, which falls into lilac mist, this house, and was curious to learn who lived here. It's curiosity, all right, that brought me, but not quite the way I put it. The fact is, I've heard the name "Mr. McGulvey" so often on the lips of the natives. "McGulvey should do something about these mosquitoes," I might overhear a dwarf mutter under his breath on a summer evening as I pass his patio. (Beneath luxuriant palms, he is reclining in a wicker chaise longue with a gin and tonic in his small brown hand.) Or a cry in the distance: "The Slob Brothers are on the loose again. Someone call McGulvey." As a tenant might send for the building superintendent when the toilet backs up.

I met the Slob Brothers, incidentally. They're enormous, and certainly frightening with their beards and spiked clubs, but quite harmless, really. But, then, no harm ever comes to you in McGulveyland. Which I figured out the second or third day, when I tripped and stepped into a hornets' nest and their stings were like a hundred kisses, given at a wedding reception, from a bunch of maiden aunts with paper-thin lips and no saliva.

Mr. McGulvey—he hasn't introduced himself yet, but I know it's Mr. McGulvey—sees through my flattery, but says nothing, only looks at me. His gray eyes are amazingly clear and penetrating. Kingly, you could almost say, though the face is a hobo face.

When I give him my name, Sherm, he nods and with a

gesture of his magnifying glass invites me to pull up a chair.

"Butterflies," he says simply, and I look at the collection on his desk. They're in a wooden box, under glass, pinned to black velvet as if they were precious gems.

No, not pinned—they're alive; they're holding still so he can examine them. Showing off their beautiful rainbow designs. I can see a feeler moving here and there, and occasionally one of the insects fidgets. Younger, probably.

"I've never seen a live butterfly collection before," I say, a little breathless, because they are absolutely gorgeous.

"Everything here is live," grunts Mr. McGulvey with pride, and his eyes crinkle at the corners.

5

The siren sounded in the middle of the night. For a moment I thought I was home and that the alarm clock had gone off by accident—it would wake Mom and there would be hell to pay, because with her schedule she needed every precious minute of her sleep. But the stumbling and cursing around me reminded me where I was, and I realized that the siren was for a dragon attack. Sir Bob and Sir Mike, on either side of me, were wriggling into their armor. I had better get into mine too, quick, and not forget my sword.

In less than two minutes, thanks to our drilling, we were down the pole and running to the parking lot, adjusting our bubble helmets as we ran. My heart hammering, I jumped into the Dart, crossed my fingers, and turned the key in the ignition. There was noise, but the car didn't start. Out of gas? I stepped harder, pumped the pedal. The car shuddered and started, but then for some reason I turned the ignition off (idiot! idiot!), which put me back to square one—worse, because now there was a strong stink of gas. This must be what they called "flooding the motor."

What was I supposed to do now? I tried to remember Mr. Bromberg on the subject, what my friends said, their older brothers, their fathers. Wait a few minutes? Floor the pedal? Which? I was close to tears. Finally, somehow—I forget what I did—the engine was going again. I took a deep breath, blew out to steady myself, said, "Here goes nothing," released the hand brake, and made what I hoped were the correct moves with the shifting—neutral, first— while stamping the pedal on the left. An ungodly rattle, a screech, a couple of lurches forward, like a clown ride in an amusement park, and the car stalled.

I was alone in the lot while my comrades were no doubt already in pitched battle risking life and limb to defend the city.

"Come on, Nelly," I pleaded with the Dart hoarsely, and tried again. After a couple more lurches and stalls, I began to get the hang of it.

A few close calls in traffic, some fist-waving in my direction, and one mortifying but minor scrape with a curb and a YIELD sign. Still, I reached the battlefield, shaky but proud of myself.

The battle, I saw, was over.

The engagement had taken place on and around a billboard overlooking a highway. The billboard originally advertised, I was told by a detective at the scene, an airline vacation to a tropical island. A squad of dragons, in the night, had come with buckets of glue and rollers on long sticks to put up their own poster. It advertised a new soda, "ZIP," which the Department of Health, working in conjunction with plainclothesmen, recently learned was a dragonproduct and—no surprise—highly toxic.

"It contains heavy metals," said the detective, putting

away his camera as the firemen hosed down the smoking ruins. "Causes nervous disorders, imbecility, insanity, and death in the space of a few months. And they aimed it at the teenage market." The detective clenched his teeth. Perhaps he had teenage children of his own. His hair was gray.

"But how could they . . ." I started to ask.

"Fronts, dummy corporations, payola," he said. "These dragons are extremely inventive and totally without scruples. They infiltrated—don't ask me how they disguised themselves—a major bottler and distributor in the area."

Sir Gardyloo was returning to his car, so I went over and asked him what had happened and if we had suffered any casualties. He was pale, did not recognize me at first, then smiled a bitter smile. (In our previous adventure together on Saraband, I remembered, he was always smiling bitter smiles. It got on my nerves.)

"Sir Josh," he said.

"Sir Josh, what? Is he hurt?" (Ah, if only I had been there! If only I had been able to fit driver's ed into my schedule a semester sooner!)

"Gone," Sir Gardyloo said.

It was hard to believe that Sir Josh, the most skilled fighter of us all, had succumbed so quickly. I asked for an account of it. Sir Gardyloo told me that they had caught the dragons red-handed and started climbing up after them on the billboard, swords drawn. The dragons didn't seem to notice them at first, which was suspicious, because the knights hadn't exactly tiptoed to the scene. Sure enough, at the last moment, when our side was almost within reach of the evil creatures, they looked down and belched fire. Sir Phil, who had shinnied up the fastest, despite his girth, was knocked clean off the billboard by a blast and landed—fortunately, otherwise that would have been the end of him—in a small backyard swimming pool, which doused the flames on him with a great hiss and an enormous puff of steam.

Sir Frank fared better. He was able to dodge the fire, grabbing a rope and swinging away, and with his sword, as he swung back like Tarzan, he knocked the bucket of glue from the grasp of his opponent. But then his opponent, laughing as dragons laugh, hit him with his long stick ending in a roller, which—

"But what happened to Sir Josh?" I asked, impatient. It wasn't pleasant, either, having to hear these feats of arms in a battle I had missed.

Sir Gardyloo sighed and pointed not anywhere on the ground, where one would expect to find the body of a fallen knight, but upward, at the billboard, or what was left of the billboard. I looked up and saw, in the one part of the dragonposter that was not charred and not obscured by smoke or by the streams of water from the firemen's hoses, a giant hand holding a giant bottle of ZIP. In the "I" on the bottle—or, rather, in place of the "I"— there was a human form, flattened, splayed, and giving off a smoke of its own, thin curling wisps of purple.

"*That* is Sir Josh?" I asked, my stomach sinking.

"It wasn't fire that got him," said Sir Gardyloo, "but treachery, dragon treachery." His voice shook. "The bottle of ZIP, which we all assumed was part of the poster, being two-dimensional . . ."

I saw it all. The dragons, observing Sir Josh's quiet prowess with the blade, must have realized that they would get nowhere with him in a fair fight, so they waited until he had climbed up and was near the bottle of their foul brew designed to cut short the lives of a whole generation of unsuspecting teenagers . . .

". . . and the stuff seemed to pour out of nowhere, and

it caught Sir Josh right in the face as he was shinnying up the rope. Then, before he could do anything—wipe the soda off, take a breath—one of the dragons swooped down and pushed him into the poster, into the bottle, and Sir Josh stuck there like it was flypaper, and the ZIP bubbled through his armor . . ."

Some men in special suits, Sir Gardyloo told me, had taken specimens for the medical examiner's at the Department of Health. The results weren't all in yet, but an unusually high concentration of dioxin was found in traces of the soda. "Sir Josh hadn't a chance."

I stepped back and raised my voice, so everyone could hear me. "I have a debt of honor to repay." This was not going to be a great speech, since I didn't have anything prepared, but what the words lacked I made up for in feeling. "It was my fault that Sir Josh perished here tonight. I swear by all that is holy, I hereby swear, mark me, that I will not return until I have drenched my sword in dragonblood to avenge, and so on."

What really burned me up was not that we had lost a knight—I didn't know the man that well, we had only shaken hands once, and he was not the sort you could get chummy with. What burned me up was that we had been unable to take out even one of their number. Ordinarily, you would expect that if one knight fell, ten or twenty dragons would be slain in the encounter.

Sir Frank came up to me with a wry face, as if to say, "That was stupid, swearing that oath. These dragons don't kill easily, in case you didn't notice."

Sir Mike also came up, wiped his sweaty, blackened brow with the back of his glove, smiled his perennial good-natured smile, and said, "Good luck, Sherm." And he gave me a friendly punch in the shoulder.

I waved, climbed back into Nelly, and after a terrible

moment—their eyes all on me as I turned the ignition and pumped the gas pedal—I lurched off into the night.

6

V. Snerk has no eyelids. His nose ends in a needle— needle as in injections. Which is appropriate, seeing as he is a doctor. *The* doctor here. Yet he's never given anyone, no matter how sick they are (not that they're ever that sick), an injection. Even the giving of pills is rare. V. Snerk relies instead on poultices and potions, and the potions are like herbal tea or gin rickey fizzes, never nasty or the kind that coat the back of your throat like clotted milk.

His lidless eyes (since we're describing him) are tiny and black, like two soaked raisins close together, and his head is spherical, white, and as bald as a hard-boiled egg without the shell.

V. is not only a doctor, he is also this world's astronomer, and has an enormous nickel-plated telescope on his back porch. It's not actually astronomy, either, that he engages in, but a sort of cross between astronomy and astrology, and sometimes he uses its results in his practice of medicine. For example, if a patient comes in with pink polka dots all over his face, V. might consult the astronomical chart with weird symbols on the wall over his diathermy machine and then excuse himself for a moment, rush out back to the telescope, and check on the position of a certain star before prescribing such-and-such a poultice or potion. The recipes are extremely exact, to three decimal places.

I don't laugh at this, because a different world requires different natural laws. What's pseudoscience on Earth could be the real thing in McGulveyland. But even if it isn't, I'm a guest here and should keep my opinions to myself.

"Yes, Sherm, what can I do for you?" says V. Snerk, not turning around.

"You probably can't help me, V.," is my reply, because I'm embarrassed and thinking how silly it was of me to come here. A cure in McGulveyland can hardly be expected to stick when I'm back home. "Back home," I say, as the doctor fiddles with whatever he's fiddling with in the metal tray by the little sink, "I have this problem."

I have a whole pile of problems, actually, but two are foremost in my mind just now: the phone problem and the blushing problem. In school they call me Red Light.

V. tests my reflexes with a rubber hammer on the knee; tapping, he mumbles something about the planet Jupiter. Then he makes a calculation on his slide rule, which I notice has letters instead of numbers, and pulls down my lower left eyelid with his thumb.

"Puberty," he concludes after a little thought. "Hormones. Capillaries. It'll pass."

That may do for the blushing problem, but the phone problem is too serious to be dismissed by a worldly-wise generalization. What if I have to call an ambulance in the middle of the night? (Scenario: Priscilla the Pill has swallowed her pillow and is turning blue. The Heimlich maneuver won't work with pillows. Thought: At the funeral, would we refer to her as Priscilla the Pillow? Mentally I chortle. Why do I hate my kid sister so much? Is this abnormal?) "But V.," I say, "if I can't get past the first letter when I'm on the phone—the first sound, that is, of the first word of the first sentence—"

"Start with the second," V. suggests.

Ignorant of him. The second letter, you see, then becomes the first. People who don't stutter don't understand. Their advice is as unhelpful as their discomfort while your stomach contracts in tighter and tighter knots and you go, "Guh . . . guh . . . guh . . ."

The real reason I came here—because I'm not stupid, I know that the phone problem and the blushing problem come with the territory of my age, like the erection problem and the acne problem. I know that there is no antidote to them but patiently waiting for twenty. The real reason I came here, the real thorn of panic in my side, is the call I have to make tomorrow.

To a girl.

V. Snerk removes his pince-nez, and although his raisin eyes have no expression, I think I see weariness in them. He says, "Maybe you should talk to Mr. McGulvey."

7

It was hard to get myself in the mood of dragonslayer. All I could think about was the spring dance. Damn officious classmates, matchmakers, Fat Clara! A lot of sophomores didn't date yet, didn't go to dances. A sophomore was a sophomore, damn it, not a junior or a senior. Out of all the guys I knew, guys my age, only Dave was going to the spring dance.

I cruised through the city, unable to concentrate on the adventure, until I saw a dragon come out of a grocery store carrying a bag. It wore a hat and a trench coat, but in the light of a street lamp I caught a glimpse of its green tail dragging on the sidewalk (they were careless, in their arrogance). The dragon saw me, but I was too quick for it. Before it could belch fire or take to the air, I jumped out of the car and cut it down with one of those sweeping diagonal slices—*shoonk!*—the samurai use in Kurosawa films starring Toshiro Mifune.

I was relieved that I had been able to make good on my oath to avenge Sir Josh by covering my blade with dragonblood. Oaths can be an awful embarrassment when time passes and your blade is still clean. There was plenty of blood, a widening pool. I had better alert the grocer, I thought, because in all likelihood the dragon had tampered with the food there. But as I stepped across the body, I saw the contents of the bag that had burst open in its fall to the pavement. A jar of baby food, broken, containing something that was the color of creamed corn. A dented can of dog food. A stalk of celery. A few apples, one of which had rolled into the gutter. A box of oatmeal. The extreme innocence of these groceries gave me pause. With a qualm of doubt, I turned the corpse over with my foot. Oh shit, it wasn't a dragon at all, it was a citizen of Cuspidor. What I had taken for a green tail was merely a strip of material—not even green—that hung in back, a torn hem in the man's coat.

Cursing, I ran back to Nelly and fortunately was able to start her up right away. But the sword, still unsheathed, had got blood all over the seat. Exhibit A. I looked around: no witnesses on the street. I drove off, Nelly kicking, and tried to think what I would tell the police if they stopped and questioned me.

8

Mr. McGulvey is gluing a chair. He looks up at me for a second when, in my explanation, I use the word "girl." He makes a pained face, as if the sun got into his eyes, and returns his attention to the chair.

The subject of girls has never before come up between us, and it dawns on me, only now, that nowhere in Mr. McGulvey's house is there a picture—a photograph, a painting, even a sketch—of the weaker sex. There is no feminine name on any of the spines or title pages of the books in his magic library. Except, of course, for Princess Martha Anne, and she doesn't count.

What does he have against women? Did one disappoint him in love many years ago? The thought is ludicrous. I just can't imagine Mr. McGulvey in a suit and tie, a flower in his lapel, moving around on a dance floor. I can't imagine him holding a little cup of pink punch as he stands by a crystal bowl and makes conversation with a demure creature in taffeta. I can't imagine him without his salt-and-pepper stubble.

Why should I burden him with an account of how Fat Clara got me into this mess? Precisely at a time when my complexion has never been so bad. And with the girl's name starting with the absolute worst letter of the alphabet, s. She'll pick up the receiver and hear, Jesus, a snake hissing on the line. No, there's no point burdening Mr. McGulvey. Let him fix his chair in peace.

This is the one area of life he can't give me pointers on.

And he knows it, too, and is grateful for my silence.

What I could use, to tell the truth, is the kind of adventure that has orgasms in it. An orgasm or two would take the steam out of the stutter demon and give me the confidence to call S.

9

The psi-fiend, they said, came from another dimension and was turning everyone communist. I took that with a grain of salt. Communism was an international movement, but I rather doubted that it was interdimensional, too. Inspector Borgenicht drove me to the house of the most recent visitation, a three-story white pseudocolonial in a development out on Georgia Avenue. Right away, even before we knocked on the door, I could smell the aura.

"A big one," I said.

He nodded. "It did quite a job on Mr. Stack. Rearranged his furniture completely."

Mrs. Stack greeted us with a wan smile, invited us in, offered us canapes and mineral water. She was middle-aged, and obviously under great strain, but holding up admirably—every hair was in place and she was able to make little sarcastic jokes as she described her ordeal.

"I first suspected something was wrong," she began, sitting opposite us on the cream-colored divan, "when Louis"—she pronounced Louis with an s—"made an uncharacteristically negative and, I must say, coarse remark regarding the new Senate Arms Appropriations Bill." She went on in that vein, making moues, for half an hour. When she got to her husband's espousal of militant black ideas and Third World guerrilla action, she faltered a little and twisted her handkerchief absently.

Inspector Borgenicht, to allay her anxiety, told her that the world's strongest psi talent (yours truly) had been prevailed upon to leave his reclusion in Scotland to take the case. "Sergeant Sherm," he said, "has tangled with beings from other planes, beings so powerful that Doctor Strange himself would dare not face them, even with *two* Tibetan amulets."

Mrs. Stark didn't seem to know who Doctor Strange was, which didn't surprise me, but she looked at me with touching urgency. "I do hope, Sergeant Sherm," she said, "that you can drive the demon out of poor Louis."

I exchanged a look with Borgenicht. He coughed uncomfortably.

"Mrs. Stark," I replied, sending out some alpha waves as I spoke, to soften the blow, "I am afraid I must tell you something that evidently has not been told you yet, and I am afraid it will distress you. You must be brave."

"I will," she said, sitting straight, hands folded in her lap. She was good at being brave. She looked me straight in the eye.

"Mr. Stark is not possessed of any demon. He is not possessed at all. He has been changed." I paused, allowing her to say:

"Then you must help us change him back, Sergeant Sherm."

With a sigh I rose and went to an ivory lamp on an end table beside a purple-and-brown crewelwork armchair. "This light is on," I said, "and I am turning it off." I pulled the chain, and the room became darker. "Now I will turn it on again," and I pulled the chain again, and the lamp was on. "You may think, Mrs. Stark," I said, turning to her, "that the light that was gone has been restored to the room. But actually that is not the case. There was a first light, and now there is a second light."

She frowned, puzzled. "I fail to see—"

"Identical the lights may be, but they are not the same. Your husband, in other words, no longer exists. His light has been extinguished."

"But he is alive!"

Mrs. Stark obviously was not attuned to the higher realities. I explained: "I can replace the person who now occupies the body of Mr. Stark with a person virtually identical to the person he was, but—"

She stood up, angry. "Really, I am not interested, Sergeant Sherm, in all this mystic mumbo jumbo. I want my

Louis back. He is not a light bulb, you know, he is a human being."

I bowed politely, schooled in politeness by my Oriental master, and exerted/extended my pneuma, which located Mr. Stark, who lay heavily sedated in a bedroom on the second floor. In a matter of seconds I moved his furniture to where it had been before, then withdrew. Inspector Borgenicht, at my side, stepped back and gasped in awe.

"I knew you were strong," he murmured, "but this . . ." Then he said, as if to himself, "Thank heaven you are on our side."

Mr. Stark—the new, third, Mr. Stark—sat up, drew aside the afghan coverlet, and got to his feet. He came down the steps slowly, evenly. His wife looked up, a touch of fright in her eyes, but her face steady, and her voice was strong when she said:

"Are you all right, Louis dear?"

"And why shouldn't I be, Henrietta?" he asked huskily, approaching us. "But I see you have guests. Can I offer you anything, gentlemen?"

Inspector Borgenicht hurriedly excused himself, took his hat, and said that unfortunately we had to be off.

I asked Mr. Stark his opinion of the new Senate Arms Appropriations Bill. He nodded, looked at me wisely, smiled, and said, "Well, it's not perfect, but this is not a perfect world, now is it?"

Mrs. Stark thanked me as I left. "I hope you won't think I was rude. All this has been so trying, you know. I haven't slept well. I didn't mean what I said about the mumbo jumbo, really I didn't."

I patted her hand and said, "Tut-tut." But on the slate walk I turned to the upper-middle-class couple standing at the front door and added, "All the clocks in your house, by the way, and all your timepieces . . ."

"Yes? Yes?" asked Mr. Stark cheerily.

"Must be rotated counterclockwise, each one, until they indicate the time they indicate now. Otherwise . . ."

"We'll do it, of course," said Mrs. Stark, waving us away—glad, I think, to be rid of us.

10

One of Sherman's jobs was to protect his kid sister at the bus stop. Bullies, Mom said. But Priscilla the Pill had always been picked on. No one liked her, had ever liked her. Even at the pre-kindergarten stage, the toddler stage, when most kids were given the benefit of the doubt, allowed to be revolting with their saggy diapers and the green coming out of their little noses, etc., forgiven this on account of their size and feebleness—even then Priscilla the Pill had had the face your fist itched to punch. It wasn't her fault; she was born that way. But it wasn't the fault, either, of the kids who hit her. They had to hit her; they couldn't help themselves. Sherman understood that. Sherman had hit her plenty, himself, in his day. Which he remembered with satisfaction. So they weren't bullies at all, they were normal, neighborhood boys, who would laugh at Sherman with the withering laughter of youthful contempt when they saw him take Priscilla the Pill's clammy little hand and escort her past them so she could reach home unhit. Their laughter would rankle, it would stay with Sherman for days. He sighed, arriving at the bus stop. Then he waited, watching the gray cattails in the swampy creek on the other side of the road. He waited for more than five minutes—the bus was late—when he could have been fighting the psi-fiend instead, or the dragons of Cuspidor, or just nosing around McGulveyland, which was a bottomless treasure chest of neat surprises. Or he could be taking a walk by himself where no one knew him and no one would look at him. Sherman didn't like to be looked at. But the bus finally appeared, the door opened, and the kids, cheering, got off. Somebody kicked Priscilla the Pill as she was stepping down. She turned around quickly, with her lower lip stuck out and her little forehead knotted with indignation—she made that face a hundred times a day—but everybody was heading home, the bus chugged away in a cloud of burnt-rubber stink, and the culprit, whoever it had been, didn't give himself away. Sherman pretended he hadn't seen. "Somebody kicked me!" Priscilla the Pill shouted up at him when he took her clammy hand as he had been instructed. He pretended not to hear that. She started to sniff—short, inward snorts—which meant that tears would be coming, big tears that would dribble down her face and drip onto the sidewalk. In his mind Sherman kicked her, like a soccer ball, across the street and into the creek, where the mud was deep under the cattails. Once, he had walked in there and sank up to his knees in the foul, sucking stuff. And now there was the laughter he had dreaded, while he led his kid sister away, she clutching her book bag. He hated it, even though these were just elementary-school boys and it didn't matter, to someone in high school, what they thought. Priscilla the Pill, clutching his hand, moaned-wept, and her tears went pat-pat-pat on the sidewalk, leaving a trail of dots behind them. Sherman looked up at the sky.

11

We got a whiff of aura on Military Road and turned left—south—on Connecticut, following it. Near Georgetown the aura became so strong, I told Inspector Borgenicht to stop. I got out and said to him through the half-open car window:

"You stay here."

He objected, of course. "I'm a fifth-level adept, certified. I can at least be of help."

I shook my head. "It's bigger than I thought. Much bigger. You wouldn't have a chance." And to myself I said: "Even I may not have a chance." But I didn't tell Borgenicht that. He was already badly spooked, though he was keeping an admirably stiff upper lip. It was better for him not to know the enormity of the threat. In his helplessness he would despair.

Giving Borgenicht a subliminal shove, I made him turn around and go back, northward, up Wisconsin Avenue, and I think he was relieved to be shoved, because even with his lesser sensitivity he must have had an inkling of the psi-fiend's power. Duty is duty, but one's skin, after all, is one's skin.

I slanted my hat lower, almost to my eyebrows, and began walking into enemy territory. I ignored the tingling, pretended to be just another pedestrian. Dozens of people here, on the street or in their houses, had had their furniture moved, and moved not a little. This was psychic mass murder on a scale I had never before encountered. There was an instance once, in Lublin, in the twelfth century, which equaled this, but that was before my time.

Gingerly, I read a few minds—gingerly, because reading controlled minds is a little like trying to touch flies caught in a web without alerting the spider. The least tug on the most distant thread can bring the monster out, big, hairy, and very fast, and in any direct confrontation-showdown I was (to change animals and metaphors) a dead duck, because this being clearly outgunned me in raw psionic wherewithal.

I would have to resort to some stratagem.

If we got out of this adventure alive, I told myself, we had to locate quickly the door to whatever dimension the intruder came from, and put a couple of good locks on it.

The minds around me, as I guessed, had been rearranged along the lines of the second Mr. Stark: that is, they were of a highly undemocratic tendency. They wanted to change everything, and change it right away, too impatient to put up with voting, speeches, compromises, and the usual wheeling and dealing. Violence, wholesale and sadistic, figured prominently in the several heads into which I peeked. The people were going to buy guns or, if they already had guns, guns of larger caliber, semiautomatic, automatic, with Teflon bullets ingeniously designed to separate flesh from bone as irreparably as possible. A few individuals were coldly pursuing plans of assassination in high places.

I went into a stationery store, bought a pack of chewing gum, went out again, and found myself on S Street. A bad omen. I had always had a problem with the letter *s*. (That witch, three adventures ago, on the Isle of Man, when my back was turned . . .)

Expecting an attack soon, I exerted/extended my pneuma, attached to it my prime persona, and sent it up and over a hill and five blocks away to Rock Creek, where I brought it to rest at the bottom of the creek, underwater. Then, using an ephemeral secondary, I erased all traces of its passage, because if this opponent turned out to be even half as smart as it was strong, it would look for a squirreled-away pneuma first thing after polishing me off.

Next, I sent a couple of projections ahead of me, down

32nd Street, like decoys, like bait. They were snuffed out with the suddenness of a thunderclap.

"Who are you?" said the psi-fiend in my ear. The aura was so overpowering—psychically, the worst bad breath in the world—that despite my experience and training, I nearly fainted.

Immediately I knew its plan. It was heading toward Capitol Hill, both geographically and politically—its objective nothing less than to paralyze, then dismember, then consume, like a giant spider, these United States.

12

Sir Josh's acid-eaten corpse ever before me, I went in search of dragonblood to rectify my mistake regarding the citizen with the groceries. Not to mention the citizen's poor dog, waiting at home with no one to feed it or take it for a walk. In my haste to redeem myself and get this stupid adventure back on the right track, I ran a red light and was pulled over by a policeman. Of course I had no registration or driver's license. I explained. He was unsympathetic.

"You won't save the city," he said, "by getting yourself killed."

I nodded, I shrugged, I waved my hands. He was right, but—

"Traffic signals are there for a reason," he said, pulling out his booklet. "And you were speeding."

"But time is running out, officer," I argued, trying to control the awful whine that kept getting into my voice. "Who knows where the dragons will strike next?"

Writing up the ticket, he gave me a sour look. "You're something of a menace yourself, Sir Scott."

"Sherm. Sir Sherm."

"People live here, you know," he lectured me. "Cuspidor is not some kind of stage for your heroics. You characters go running around in your capes and helmets having a good time—"

"We get killed!"

"—and I wouldn't be surprised if you cause more harm than those so-called dragons of yours."

"So-called?!" Speechless, I gasped.

"Yes, and what's all that blood from?"

"Blood?"

"Blood, do you think I'm blind? In my job I see blood all the time. I know what blood is, buster. It's on your costume—"

"Tunic."

"—and shoes, and—what's this?—in the car, too."

I told him the whole story, too demoralized by now to try to make up something.

"You see?" said the policeman with a triumphant grimace. "Just like I said. Playing knights and dragons, and you end up killing innocent bystanders."

"It's not a game, officer. I don't know how you can think it's a game. Anyway, the man may be only wounded. I didn't take his pulse."

"No, of course you didn't. . . ." And he handed me the ticket. "In too much of a hurry, weren't you? Let the beggar bleed to death. Let the chips fall where they may. You knights are thoughtless and irresponsible, and if I had my way, you'd be disbarred and your swords would be taken from you. And another thing, mister: you didn't indicate a turn two blocks back. Made the white Chevy jam on its brakes. Where in the hell did you learn how to drive? Now, I'm going to tell you this. One more citation,

Sir Scott or whatever your heroic name is, and you won't get off with just a fine."

I started up Nelly and limped away, wanting to hide my face in the darkness, since it was redder—curse my hormones! curse my capillaries!—than the cursed traffic light. Christ, when was I going to grow up?

13

Mr. McGulvey, legend has it, once lived on Earth like other mortals. He even went to school. He even worked in an office and wore a tie. Something, anyway, disgusted him so much that he came here. And never went back. I don't question him about his past, of course, but sometimes Old Corduroy, who's been here longer than anybody, even before McGulveyland was McGulveyland, will slip in a quick little half-allusion between sentences, hardly noticeable, while we're playing cards or throwing British darts in his cavern den.

"McGulvey, well, you know, the taxes," he said on one occasion.

Did that mean that Mr. McGulvey, back in the days when he lived among men, decided he didn't want to pay his taxes any longer? And, if so, was this in protest against government spending, the defense budget, the millions and billions of dollars going into ICBMs? Although there probably were no ICBMs then. But who knows? The time lines are totally different between the two worlds, between here and there. I can be in a baseball game at gym, for example, standing in weeds out in boring left field, and phase here, spend a couple of days, have an adventure, too, and when I phase back, the same guy is at bat, only maybe it's two-and-two now instead of one-and-one.

Did they put Mr. McGulvey in jail, like Thoreau (according to Mr. Stammler, who doesn't always get his facts straight)? I make up a story like that in my mind—fuzzy but heroic—all built on a few words that may have meant something entirely different, or even nothing at all. Old Corduroy is not exactly senile, but his great age has made him . . . odd. I think that when your head gets too full of experience, it starts shorting out, like an overloaded motor.

For example, I never knew a history teacher whose eyes didn't go blurry every five minutes or so.

Old Corduroy's face is covered with wrinkles that are like tiny fracture lines in a glazed pot, and he has wattles under his chin. Yet he dresses like a schoolboy, with shorts, buckles on his shoes, and huge black buttons. He often carries a book under his arm (a reader), chews bubble gum, and likes to play old-fashioned practical jokes, such as putting tacks on chairs or balancing buckets of water over doors. He giggles, and he has a marble collection.

Squeak once told me that Old Corduroy goes back as far as Eden or the Crusades. I made a polite murmur of amazement, but chuckled to myself. Yet Eden or the Crusades may mean something quite different from what it means back home. You have to be careful, in McGulveyland, not to dismiss as absurd what people tell you. I remember, when I was here only a few days, some washerwoman came running through, pulling nervously on her bonnet and exclaiming that the sky was falling. I laughed—but damned if it didn't fall. No one was hurt, of course, though there was some damage to the hibiscuses and sunflowers in people's backyard gardens. A deafening crash, and big blue shards everywhere; that was all. It was quickly cleaned up—I helped, too, with broom and dustpan—and a new sky was put in the next day.

I'm really not all that interested in the past. It's unimportant to me what Mr. McGulvey did twenty or a hundred and twenty years ago. The present suffices, an endless and easy present in which to enjoy his company. He's not going anywhere. There are no business trips a person has to take here, and nobody dies.

14

It was with ozone, hydrocarbons, and free radicals of sulfur—an unspeakably vile mixture—that the dragons got Sir Bob. The battle took place in the amusement park on the other side, north, of the Cuspidor municipal reservoir. Sir Bob was felled in the fun house by a sudden jet of the poison gases from below (that old joke of making women's skirts fly upward). He was dead before he hit the planks, because his helmet had not been completely sealed at the neck. A lesson for the rest of us.

Sir Bob was a decent, likable guy, with his ready smile and open, Dan-Aykroyd face, and I hated to see him go.

Sir Phil was incapacitated by an attack of asthma brought on by a whiff of the gas, and Sir Gardyloo got lost in the mirror maze, but Sir Mike and I flushed a dragon from one of the control rooms and hacked at it with our swords before it could take to the air or spit anything harmful. Our first kill, and about time.

Meanwhile, Sir Frank did his Tarzan bit on the rollercoaster scaffolding—the man didn't appear to mind heights. A couple of times he came extremely close to breaking his neck or getting blowtorched to a crisp, but he always managed to dodge and recover his balance at the last second. He didn't take out any dragons, but his action was helpfully diversionary.

(As for Sir Gawain, if you're keeping count, he was home, at the firehouse, with a bad cold.)

Buoyed by our success, Sir Mike and I ran out onto the main promenade, where we saw a dragon duck into an arcade. We followed, running in a half-crouch, our eyes searching the paint-peeled belfries and minarets above for possible snipers. The arcade was deserted, but out of the corner of my eye I thought I saw something green flick in the vicinity of the fortune-teller's booth. I pointed with my sword, we ran there, and Sir Mike swept aside the entrance curtain.

The fortune-teller, a hooded Gypsy, sat at her crystal ball and did not look up, as if absorbed in some intricate vision of the future. Sir Mike pulled up a chair opposite her while I poked around in the closet and behind and under the sofa bed.

"Tell me my fortune," he said, squinting warily, gripping his sword, whose blade—like mine—still smoked from dragonblood.

The Gypsy bent lower over her crystal ball and whispered: "Are you police?"

"Knights," said Sir Mike.

"What do you seek?"

"Dragons."

"There are no dragons here," whispered the Gypsy, suddenly very hoarse. "Only a poor fortune-teller."

"Dragons can disguise themselves," I said, behind her.

She flinched at my voice and seemed to shrink. "I am not a dragon," she croaked, trembling.

"Then tell me my fortune," said Sir Mike. I could see the muscles in his jaw working. The air in the room was foul.

"Tomorrow," began the Gypsy in a singsong, swaying

from side to side, "you will depart on a long journey, meet a stranger, find a treasure . . ."

"She's fake, it's obvious," I said, and we cut her down. This now evened the score two to two: two dragons for Sir Josh and Sir Bob.

Our eyes stung during the funeral, the air quality was so bad, and Sir Phil experienced such difficulty breathing that I had to leave the cemetery in the middle of the service to take him to an allergist, who, after we sat in the waiting room for more than an hour, gave him a shot of Adrenalin and then one of those bronchial dilator inhalers, which helped a lot.

15

Sherman had to clean the toilet. This was the job he hated most. It wasn't that the toilet smelled that bad—it smelled a little—it was the idea. To have to touch the seat where people peed and crapped and farted, and touch the bowl with little spots of yellow and brown. In order to scrub those spots off, you had to bring your face close, down, right up to the bowl, like kissing someone's behind. Who else at Whitney cleaned the family toilet? (Not counting girls, of course, because girls did everything their mothers did—the smiling little homemakers—probably even this.) Why couldn't Sherman's mother clean the toilet like other mothers? Sharing the work—she lectured—dividing the responsibilities. "I get home at six-thirty," she said. "I don't have the energy." And Priscilla the Pill was, of course, too young. We all have to chip in, Sherman. Mom put in extra hours, and on weekends often brought home work, all kinds of folders and pads and booklets in her briefcase. It gave her a headache, but she toughed it out.

She had deep vertical frown marks over her nose, permanent furrows that made her look older than she was, ten
years older, sometimes twenty years older. Sherman wished
she would have the furrows cosmetic-surgically removed
and get married and let her husband—some dumb, good-
natured type with a big smile and nodding all the time—
bring home the money and get the headaches. Then Sherman wouldn't have to put his face in the toilet bowl
anymore. It wasn't natural for a boy to put his face in a
toilet bowl. It wasn't good for his manhood. But Mom
argued: college tuition, not only his but Priscilla's, too,
eventually. That was why they had to swallow their pride
and watch every penny. "We can't afford maids." Dave
never washed a dish in his life, let alone a toilet, and
would have blinked in disbelief if anybody suggested such
a thing. A boy's hands were for baseball, for tying knots in
ropes, for tinkering with black-greasy nuts and bolts in the
guts of old Buicks.

16

As I feared, the magic library has not a thing even
remotely pornographic. I check while Mr. McGulvey is
out in the closed-in porch that overlooks the gorse. On the
table there he's spread out some notes on hydrangea—in
innumerable looseleaf notebooks—because someone in the
Valley has a hydrangea problem and wrote to him. Mr.
McGulvey is super-scrupulous about responding to letters
that ask for advice, and I've known him sometimes to take
a whole week to draft an answer. So he will be a while.

I look through every volume on every shelf—that is, on
every fiction shelf. There's a whole wall of nonfiction
that I don't bother with.

No women's legs, no breasts. No grass skirts or gyrating brown bellies. The occasional female character is invariably chalk white, in whalebone, and so starched from neck to toe that she can't draw in air enough to raise her voice. That's why she enunciates carefully: everything otherwise would be an unintelligible whisper. I have an aunt like that, in Chicago. Her face is caked with powder and she has a parakeet for a pet. Binky.

Riffling the pages for smut, I keep looking over my shoulder at the door, which has been left innocently ajar so Mr. McGulvey won't suspect. I really shouldn't be doing this. It's shameful, in such a clean, wholesome place.

What if he appears suddenly at the door with an "Ahem"? No, Mr. McGulvey would never go "Ahem." He would just stand there and look at me turn beet-red as I babbled that I was only, er, browsing. He would see through that right away, but say nothing.

Still, at this point in my private life, I need . . . it's only normal biology, after all, to need . . .

It's the spring dance, I think, that's got me wrought up and put my thoughts on this track. Why, the other night I even found myself dirty-fantasizing about S, who's not that pretty, who probably doesn't like me (why should she?), and whom I'm supposed to call this evening (damn, damn) because Fat Clara told her I would.

But Mr. McGulvey's books don't help, and when they change—because every week they change—I'm sure that not one of them will change into anything I can use for an orgasm adventure.

Unless he keeps such books in a separate place, under lock and key . . . Whistling, nonchalant, I walk about the house, go from room to room, quietly and unobtrusively rapping panels with my knuckles, looking for secret com-

partments, hidden doors to hidden studies. My palms are
sticky with sweat.

17

The moment the psi-fiend began shoving its huge hairy
paws into my brain to rearrange my furniture—and parrying him would have been like trying to wrestle with a
train—I self-destructed and woke, in fish form, at the
bottom of Rock Creek, near the mill. I heard the slow
plosh-plosh-plosh of the paddle wheel, while overhead, on
the surface, green-blue bubbles and froth floated by, with
occasional swirls probably caused by the little waterfall
half a mile upstream, although the rocks also made eddies
in the current, eddies and bubbles. It was so peaceful, so
soothing, to watch the floating and the swirling, that for a
few minutes—a few hours?—I did not even bother to ask
myself who I was and what I was doing here.

Someone tugged on my subcortical intercom. A friend,
judging by the rhythm. But in these fetal alpha-dormancies,
which are entered into only as a last-ditch defense—which
means, of course, that the danger is the direst—one can-
not be too careful, so I countertugged, ready to break the
connection (pre-connection, that is) at the first false beat of
the reply. But the other party knew the code, all of it. It
had to be Hsün Hsien Wu Chang. Smiling, I picked up
the receiver (figuratively, for I was in a state of handlessness).

"Peace to my august mentor," I said. "What's up?"

"In over your head, aren't you?" said old Hsün, who
wasn't born yesterday.

"It would appear so," I admitted, as a piece of bark,
rotating, gracefully slid past—from my perspective—be-

tween the crown of a tree and a cumulous cloud, like a lazy bird.

"Is it looking for you?" asked Hsün.

I sighed. "I haven't checked yet." I wasn't anxious to send out a secondary to scout. A secondary could reveal my position if the enemy was rooting around in the neighborhood, or if he had secondaries of his own hunting for a squirreled-away pneuma. If that happened, I'd be in a battle again, immediately, and this time without a backup persona. It would be total curtains then for Sergeant Sherm.

"Want me to check for you?"

"No, no, I wouldn't think of dragging you into this," I said. Hsün had retired, after centuries of crossing psychic swords with unholy, unnameable things, and now ran a Szechwan restaurant in downtown Invergordon. It was there that I met him . . .

[FLASHBACK]

As I looked at the stained menu, deliberating, the waiter, a short, stooped man with only a few hairs combed across his bald head, waited with typical Oriental impassiveness at my elbow. "Mu shu pork," I said finally. He nodded and took the menu, but before he could leave, I couldn't resist remarking: "Do you get much business? I wouldn't think there would be a great demand for Chinese cuisine here in the north of Scotland."

But the waiter only nodded again, as if not understanding English, or at least not my American accent, and withdrew to the kitchen.

[END OF FLASHBACK]

. . . and there that he introduced me to the Seven Occult Ways and set me up, when my training and initiation were completed, in the mossy, misty, ancestral hold overlooking Loch Shin.

"All right," said the great sage. "But I think it's time I told you about the noumenal umbra."

"Come again?"

"Did you ever wonder what that little red button was for, on the back of your digital watch?"

18

No Princess Martha Anne, cowled but in armor from neck to toe, was going to bail Sherman out of this tight spot of tight spots. No friendly Slob Brother—like Glob or Gob, three placid blue eyes blinking—was going to lift Sherman onto his broad twenty-feet-off-the-ground shoulder and carry him with huge strides out of this excruciating predicament. It was less than two minutes to nine now, and the phone was staring our hero in the face. He was so nervous, he was sick, green, clammy, shaking, as he had been—exactly—when they wheeled him three years ago into the operating room, where under a blinding light the surgeons all turned to face him, wearing white masks and holding long shiny silver scissors in their rubber gloves to take out his appendix. It would be awful beyond words, this phone call, but he had to go through with it, there was no choice. Shaking, he dialed. When the mother answered, he could not get past the c in "Could I speak to . . .?" and the stutter demon was so much in control, so damned quick, that switching to "I would like to speak to . . ." didn't help. Sherman managed to stumble past the *w* of "would," but the *l* of "like," usually a sound that gave him no trouble, stopped him like the coils of an anaconda. After seven luh's, he gave up—but nevertheless, dripping with sweat, unexpectedly identified himself, because the mother helped by finally asking, "Who is this?" He got out a whole sentence then, answering before the demon could grab him again: "This is Sherman Potts." The mother, after listening to snake-hissing a while, got the idea that he wanted to speak to Susan. Sherman didn't want to speak to Susan, he wanted to die and be buried somewhere far away, beyond the sea, without a marker, because this was a hundred times worse than he had thought it would be, he had never in his life been so stricken, and the sweat poured from his face like a downspout in a heavy rain. Susan, knowing about the whole arrangement from Fat Clara, pretend-conversed with him. The way you talked into a phone on stage, in a play. But there were a few things she didn't know beforehand and had to ask and wait for an answer, such as, "When will you pick me up?" And since Sherman was faced with saying "seven," there was more snake-hissing. Sherman thought, "I'm a cripple. She's going out with a cripple. She must be desperate. Somebody canceled on her at the last minute and she doesn't care how she gets to the spring dance. She would go with a monkey." Another necessary question to ask, since Susan knew he didn't have a car: How was he going to pick her up? Answer: Dave would provide transportation, Dave had his license, a car, he too was going, it would be a double date. To get all this out took forever, Sherman steering clear of treacherous sounds as best he could and Susan waiting patiently or sometimes guessing tactfully. Sherman thought, "She pities me," and that made him feel so pitiful, tears came to his eyes. When at last the business was taken care of—by then it was nine-thirty-nine—he suddenly felt limp but tremendously relieved, not shaking anymore. He was anxious to hang up, started saying goodbye, but evidently Susan thought they ought to make a little personal conversation now, as if they had gone through this hell not on account of Fat Clara but were actually boyfriend and girlfriend. She asked him what his hobbies were. Sherman said he guessed he didn't have a hobby. "No hobby?" asked Susan, shocked. "How can you not have a hobby? Everybody has a hobby." Sherman said he just didn't have the time. Susan laughed. "Come on, Sherman," she said, "of course you have the time. I mean, you're not one of those super A-students who do nothing but study. Or those student-government social types who are in a dozen school clubs and all so stuck-up. God, I hate them." Sherman had a hobby, all right, but his hobby was nobody's business, and suddenly he wanted to punch this stupid, normal girl in the mouth or hold her head underwater for an hour, until the bubbles stopped.

Chapter Two

• 1 •

Well, I know I shouldn't, but I'm off to look for the snake in the Garden of Eden. There has to be a sex book somewhere in this world. Mr. McGulvey, who sees through everything, won't see through my scheme, because sex is his blind spot, women his Achilles heel. When I find the forbidden fruit, I'll sneak it into his library, hide it in that little dusty slot behind the walnut credenza, and he won't be the wiser.

McGulveyland, geographically, is huge, about the size of Russia or possibly even the entire continent of Asia. So I will probably be gone a while. I pack my suitcase carefully, remembering to take insect repellent and sufficient change for tolls, Laundromats, and to make phone calls in emergencies.

Shaking hands with Mr. McGulvey—and his hand is big and warm—I thank him for his hospitality and tell him I'm going exploring. Which is true. Actually, this is something I've wanted to do for some time. Mr. McGulvey nods, as if having expected all along that I would be going exploring, and invites me to have lunch with him first.

Unceremoniously, on the small kitchen table, without plates, he puts down slices of Wonder Bread, spreads mayonnaise on them with a rubber spatula, and deals out bologna slices, one per slice of bread. A limp leaf of lettuce, green-gray at the edges, goes on top of each bologna slice, then two halves are put together face-to-face to make one sandwich, so you have: bread, mayonnaise, bologna, double lettuce, bologna again, mayonnaise, and bread. Since the sandwich is picked up without being cut, and the bread is not toasted, one needs both hands. It tastes fabulous. The secret, I think, is in not using a plate, in letting the food rest right on the table with the crumbs of other meals.

Mr. McGulvey says nothing during this send-off lunch in my honor. He chews thoughtfully. I watch his jaw stubble move up and down. We eat three sandwiches each, and leave the other five on the table. Perhaps he will have them for supper or snacks. It doesn't matter. Food doesn't spoil in McGulveyland. Mom, of course, would have fifty fits if I did anything like that at home.

V. Snerk, as I'm walking down the slate path past his place, sticks his head out a window and asks me if I wouldn't mind taking a vial of something to a cousin of his in Barnett-by-the-Gulf.

"And where is Barnett-by-the-Gulf?" I ask, amused at the request. Because if the stuff is medicine, and I can't find the town (and have you ever tried to ask directions in McGulveyland? and there are no maps), his cousin will languish in what might be a serious condition.

"You can't possibly miss it," says V.

"Don't you think it would be better if you mailed the vial to him?" I suggest.

But V. is already tossing it to me. Fortunately I am able to catch it. He shakes his egglike head. "Can't talk now, sorry. I have a patient." And the blinds are dropped back into place.

He hasn't even given me the name of his cousin.

2

The silver spaceship stood at the center of the jungle colony, vertical and proud upon its great fins, pointing at the stars we left, a constant reminder of Home. I sighed and let the blinds drop back into place. The music of the crickets and tree frogs (of course they were not crickets and tree frogs, but that was what we called them), usually so soothing, throbbed in my head now like an incessant question. Who would have predicted this problem, this peril?

Another sleepless night of pacing and consulting the printouts. We had everything going for us. A close-knit community of pioneers, the finest scientists and first-rate technicians, a world optimal in terms of ecosphere, climate, and the absence of intelligent life-forms. Fourth planet of Lambda Eridani, seven hundred light-years from Earth, and safely off the beaten path—a good ten parsecs from the nearest trading station of the Guild or any transgalactic lane. A perfect spot, in short, to start over again, and a paradise for a naturalist. Millions of new species—no, billions.

It all began, I mused, with the chocolate cake. Scrig had baked it to celebrate the anniversary of our landing. For chocolate he used the long black beans of the *lakol* plant, which lived in an odd symbiosis with the spiny mudworms on the banks of the Pickle, the only river that went through this part of the jungle. (We had named it the Pickle because of its dark-green color and the bubbles that continually disturbed its surface. Also, the water did have a salty-sour taste.) You could tell the difference between chocolate and *lakol* right away, but *lakol* wasn't a bad substitute: imagine chocolate with a hint of orange peel. A hot drink made of the stuff was very popular in the colony.

Cory and the other officers had opened a bottle of Earth champagne and were toasting me—"And here's to old Commander Sherm, who got us here in one piece"—when there was a call from the pump facility at North End, a broken gasket, so I had to copter over there and be the authority figure, give a couple of orders—obvious, commonsense directions—because otherwise they would panic. It wasn't healthy, I told myself, for everyone to be so dependent on me. We were no longer in space, traveling from unknown to unknown, where crises came roaring out of nowhere and required instant decisions. The colonists should begin thinking for themselves, standing on their own two feet. I would have to wean them from me.

When I returned, three hours later, to my cabin, the party was over, but Cory had written a message and placed it by the phone: "We finished the bubbly—sorry, sir, couldn't help it—but there's a piece of chocolate cake for you in the fridge."

Except there wasn't.

I thought that extremely peculiar. Cory was not the type to play practical jokes, and none of the officers—not Watkins, not Morgan, not Pliscou—would have dreamed of filching a piece of chocolate cake, or anything else, from me. They practically worshiped me, though they tried not to show it. No, they had definitely left me a piece of chocolate cake, and it had been the biggest piece. I knew my men.

Where, then, was the cake?

I made discreet inquiries the next day. Buster, that old wrinkled salt who knew everybody's business in the colony and, before that, on the ship, was not even aware that Scrig had baked a chocolate cake. He was hurt that he hadn't been let in on it. "I can see it was a special occasion, among the officers," he said, chewing the stem of his corncob pipe, "but Scrig could at least have told me." I clapped Buster on the back, which made him feel better instantly, and gave him a task (he was in charge of supplies) having to do with spare parts and the machine shop at West End, which took his mind completely off the slight. Psychology.

Poindexter, our curmudgeonly exobiologist, harrumphed at the suggestion that a life-form indigenous to New Batavia (what we were obliged to name the planet, for reasons too complicated to go into here) may have opened the fridge and made off with the cake. "First of all," he said, "to open the fridge you'd need an opposable thumb, and we haven't come across anything remotely like that here. Secondly, there's not an animal on the planet, as far as we know, larger than a mouse."

"Isn't that odd?" I asked.

"It's damned odd," Poindexter growled.

What possibilities remained? Was there a thief among us? I consulted Hotchkiss, the colony shrink, who reminded me a little of V. Snerk, his eyes were so close together, but he drew a blank on the question of social pathology cropping up in our midst. "It's a bit early," he said, "for deviations to manifest themselves. We're still very much a close-knit pioneer community. It's only been a year, and we haven't expanded much."

"We haven't, because the trees in this jungle are difficult to cut down," I reminded him, "what with their unusually dense xylem. And they have a way of growing back quickly, because of their extensive root system and amazing hormones."

He nodded. There were trees pushing up through almost everyone's living room. It was a nuisance.

"Also," Hotchkiss went on, "if there is a thief in the

colony, one would expect him to go after the emeralds, for example"—enormous green gems unearthed last month by a scouting expedition in mountainous terrain near the equator in New Batavia's other hemisphere—"or go after some of our invaluable souvenirs from Home, such as a bottle of French champagne. One would not expect him to break and enter for the sake of a simple wedge of *lakol* chocolate cake."

"True," I said, and let the matter drop.

But then Barkley, a nuclear engineer, reported the disappearance of a box of cereal from his wife's cupboard—not of the box, that is, but of the contents of the box: locally made flakes reminiscent of Wheaties. And Havilland, the navigator, reported the disappearance of a sack of "yams." And so on and so forth, until every household, every cabin had been hit.

We knew we were up against something serious, however, only with the LoBianco Incident. The LoBianco family had set up a picnic by the Pickle, inviting the Cuthbertsons and the Slonimskis. A scenic view, a sunny day, a long table filled with baskets of fried "chicken," plates of roast "beef," bowls of potato salad (real potatoes, these, planted from Terran stock) and "corn" chips, and a variety of mouth-watering breads, cakes, and cookies. More than enough food for the dozen people there. Little Billy LoBianco heard a splash in the river and the silver glimmer of one of those funny squeak-fish, so he pointed and shouted, "Look!"

When they turned back to the table a second later, maybe two seconds later, it was completely bare.

3

Sir Gawain got it next, through the most despicable kind of dragon treachery: murdered by the thing he loved most, pizza. This was clearly in revenge for the dragons' double loss at the amusement park.

He had been going regularly to the corner pizzeria after lights-out, though Sir Frank took him to task for it. "How can you sleep with your stomach full of that garbage?" the older knight lectured him—because Sir Gawain liked "everything" pizzas, and then would pile garlic salt, oregano, and hot pepper on top of that, from the shakers there. He could consume an entire pizza by himself in the middle of the night. I joined him a couple of times, but found it hard to keep my eyes open. Without a full eight hours of sleep, I wasn't good for much the next day. Sir Gawain sat across from me in the booth and put away slice after slice, grinning all the while, and the more he ate, the more he grinned. A simple soul.

It was the regularity of it that did him in. The dragons, apparently, had spies everywhere, and kept track of our comings and goings. One morning, when we got up to drill, Sir Gawain lay deathly pale on his bed, his eyes fixed on the ceiling.

"I told you you'd get indigestion," said Sir Frank angrily.

"Wait," said Sir Mike, "it's more than indigestion." And he went and closed all the blinds and turned off Sir Gardyloo's reading lamp.

Sure enough, in the dimness Sir Gawain glowed.

"Radiation poisoning," whispered Sir Mike.

"How do you know?" asked Sir Frank.

"I read a book on the subject. You can tell by the skin. The pores."

"Doesn't the hair fall out?"

"In about a week. But he won't last that long. I'd say he was exposed to something on the order of ten-to-the-six roentgens."

"That's a fatal dose?"

"It would be fatal for a school of whales. There's nothing we can do for him."

Sir Frank called an ambulance, and Sir Gawain, not blinking, was taken to the Cuspidor City Hospital. Sir Mike and I, meanwhile, investigated the pizzeria. From his cape Sir Mike produced a Geiger counter and ran it over the premises. I questioned the owner, the two waitresses, the dishwasher. The owner swore up and down that his place was clean. It had recently been certified A-OK by the Department of Health (he showed me the certificate, stamped and dated). He used only the finest ingredients.

"No other customers were taken ill?" I asked.

But Sir Mike gestured me over. The Geiger counter was aimed and click-clacking like a machine gun: the culprit was the pepperoni.

We got the name and address of the supplier of the pepperoni, and drove there, our fingers itching to use our swords. The factory, a red-brick building with an old faded sign, PERFECT PEPPERONI, was situated across the street from another firehouse, another company of knights. We decided to warn them first, in case any of them also went in for "everything" pizzas. And perhaps, too, we hoped that they might want to join us in the raid. The more the merrier. But the knight in charge shrugged dispiritedly. "We've given up," he said. "There are only two of us left, me and Sir Dave. Look, my hair's already turning gray, and I'm not thirty yet."

"That might be from radiation," remarked Sir Mike.

So we girded our loins, entered the pepperoni building, and were ushered into the manager's office. The manager swore up and down that he didn't hire dragons. "I'm not in the business of poisoning people," he said. Sir Mike thought a while and asked to see the assembly line. The assembly line was so noisy, you couldn't hear yourself think. Long skinny sausages were chopped into the familiar red-brown coin pieces, and then the pieces were packaged. We kept our eyes peeled for telltale green among the workers, and Sir Mike unobtrusively used his Geiger counter. Nothing.

"Perhaps they're all in on it," I said to him, drawing him aside. "Humans paid to do dragonwork."

Sir Mike shook his head. "A few they could pay. The manager, the pizzeria owner, but not everyone. There are maybe fifty employees here. And it's not just a question of money. Most people, Sherm, aren't Judas material."

"You're an optimist."

If only we could unmask a dragon. Then Sir Mike, using his muscles, would pick it up bodily and hurl it into the chopping machine, which in a trice, with a big coughing sound, would make hundreds of green, toxic pepperoni pieces. What a great scene that would make! I wanted action. Standing and watching a noisy pepperoni assembly line was boring. And the dragons were ahead, 3–2 . . .

Finally we drove to the hospital to see how poor Sir Gawain was doing. He had been put in Intensive Care. Sir Gardyloo, with a pitying expression, sat at the bedside holding the dying knight's hand. Actually—the nurse informed us—Sir Gawain had already expired. It gave me an eerie feeling to see the man's face still glowing, like a moon, on the hospital pillow.

4

As a fish, I headed downstream, because Rock Creek fed the Potomac. At the Potomac the water was warmer and not as clean, but I wasn't here to take environmental notes. I bore left, south, and passed under a couple of bridges. In the shadow of the third bridge I turned left again, east, into the tidal basin where the Jefferson Memorial was, if my memory served me correctly. The showdown, I knew, would be at the far end of the Mall: the Capitol building. The psi-fiend would be massing its minions there for an attack on Congress.

Strange, I reflected, that here I was readying myself for a duel-to-the-death, and most likely it would be *my* death, since grappling with this monster was a bit like trying to move a planet from its orbit using only judo, though on certain occult planes judo, essentially the principle of leverage, was able to—and who was it who said, "Give me a place to stand, and I can move the earth"? I was having difficulty finishing thoughts. A sign of nerves.

Reciting a Tantric mantra, I took a deep breath—or whatever analogous thing fish do—and began my reconstitution, changing from pneuma to umbra, as my august mentor had advised. I hoped it would work.

Strange—I returned to my reflection, determined this time to complete it, because I really had to get a grip on myself. Self-control would be all-important in the encounter with this wholesale mental furniture rearranger from dimension X.

Strange, that here I was putting my life on the line for a nation I had scornfully renounced. Middle-class America, urban decay, suburban sprawl, the shopping malls, the materialism.

It was the materialism that had sent me fleeing to the mossy, misty, ancestral hold overlooking Loch Shin in the north of Scotland. And yet here I was, after an invitation—a call for help—from Inspector Borgenicht, playing Nathan Hale or Patrick Henry, whom I had got mixed up on Mr. Stammler's test last week, but that had nothing to do with this adventure.

The umbra identity I chose was a hot-dog vendor pushing his cart beneath a yellow-and-orange striped umbrella. For the time it took me—took him—to reach the Capitol building, Sergeant Sherm would not exist; not even the deepest psychic probe would notice him, because he would be noumenally ineffable and no more sentient—less sentient, in fact—than the sidewalk beneath his feet.

America, I supposed, did mean something to me after all, the land of the free and the home of the brave, and the moment I materialized from thin air I pushed the little red button on the back of my digital watch, knowing that my next conscious moment would be—

Battle! I was surrounded by bomb-throwing assassins. Before they could throw their bombs at me, I rang my bicycle bell on the side of the cart and offered them hot dogs: hot dogs with mustard, ketchup, chopped onions, hot dogs with relish or sauerkraut; hot dogs, than which nothing is more American; hot dogs evocative of baseball games, the circus, carnivals in the summer, the Fourth of July, parades and flags and marching bands and fire trucks with hook, ladder, and handlebar mustache. Hot dogs that a man can eat anytime, not just for lunch or supper, and anywhere, on the street, out in a field, at the beach, and they're not expensive, either, and therefore: hot dogs, the food of liberty, fraternity, equality.

Oops, wrong country, France. The terrorists—all creatures of the psi-fiend, whose aura was strong enough to knock over a barn, so it had to be in our midst, in other words a stone's throw from the Senate and the marble steps and statues of our forefathers—raised their bombs and weapons again. Their eyes were unseeing and burned like coals, reminding me of a zombie movie I had once gone to at a drive-in with my cousin Sammy and which still gave me nightmares.

But hold on, the French built the Statue of Liberty! (Thank heaven for Mr. Stammler, good for something after all!) Hot dogs and the Statue of Liberty, there was potency in that. The smell of them sizzling on the grill, anyway, ideology aside (but that was the whole point, hot dogs were aside of ideology), was irresistible, it took the murder out of the hearts of the enemies of democracy around me. They started fishing in their pockets for change, opening their wallets. Suddenly they realized they were hungry.

The psi-fiend, enraged, came down on me like a ton of bricks—but I winked out and hid under the umbra, so all it found was an ordinary hot-dog vendor selling hot dogs to a crowd by the reflecting pool. Old Hsün certainly knew his stuff: this trick was worth a dozen Tibetan amulets.

5

Barnett-by-the-Gulf, it turns out, is a place that keeps cropping up no matter where you go. You're in the mountains? Turn the corner of a mountain path—the kind where there's no shoulder, just a sheer perpendicular drop always a few feet to your left as you follow the snaking curves upward—and *voilà*, Barnett-by-the-Gulf lies nestled in a valley, complete with the gulf and white-sailed skiffs on its blue-green water. Or you're in the middle of an endless desert, nothing but dunes and cacti for miles

and miles in all directions? Beyond the next ridge, without
fail, is Barnett-by-the-Gulf, not a bit different, the yellow-
and-orange stucco houses the same, the water and the
skiffs the same, the barbershop pole turning the way it
always turns, slowly and steadily. . . .

To what ocean or sea does the gulf belong? And what
kind of ocean or sea can it be, to have arms reaching into
every corner, no matter what the terrain, of this vast
continent? I see it in the distance, a blue haze on the
horizon, and it looks like a perfectly normal ocean or sea,
not one that defies the most fundamental principles of
topology. But this is McGulveyland. Throw away your
maps, your compasses, O traveler, for they are useless
here.

When I looked at a train schedule, I saw that whether I
headed north, south, east, or west, one of the stops was
Barnett-by-the-Gulf. So naturally I got off here, wanting
to get my errand with the vial out of the way.

"Where is everyone?" I ask a native, a gentleman in a
summer suit and turban.

He smiles. "It is Tuesday." As if that explains why the
streets are empty and there are only one or two skiffs out
on the water, although the weather is perfect. (I am not
yet aware that the weather is always perfect at Barnett-by-
the-Gulf.)

"Oh. Is Tuesday a kind of Sabbath for you?" I hazard.

The native smiles, as if appreciating the joke I have
made, and takes me by the arm and leads me to a table of
a sidewalk café, where I am served a fluffy, golden-brown
omelet in a shallow bowl. The omelet, when I cut into it
with a fork, is filled with molten cheddar cheese sprinkled
with pieces of purple onion and green pepper.

It is the custom in McGulveyland, I learn later, to feed
someone before he departs as well as upon his arrival.

This is the reason tourists, who are constantly departing and arriving, are so corpulent. Most of the people in my train car, I recall, had trouble sitting down and getting up again, and were generally out of breath.

"I'm looking for a cousin of a certain V. Snerk," I tell the native, my mouth full of omelet, and begin to describe V. Snerk, assuming that this relative may also have close-set, raisinlike eyes, a needle nose, and a hairless head that resembles a hard-boiled egg out of its shell. The native, smiling, holds up his hand to stop me.

"Here," he says, "everyone is a cousin of V. Snerk."

"That will make my search difficult," I say, "since V. neglected to give me the name of his cousin as I was leaving."

The native, smiling, shakes his head, as if my humor amazes him. "In Barnett-by-the-Gulf," he explains at last, "no one has a name."

I wonder if he is pulling my leg. How can a town conduct its business, whatever its business is, without names for its citizens? How would you differentiate between them, particularly if they all looked alike, being related? But this native in the turban bears no family resemblance to V. Snerk. He looks, if anything, like Mr. Bromberg, my driver's ed teacher. So I'm getting suspicious. Perhaps the rule, in Barnett-by-the-Gulf, is to lie whenever you're asked a question.

With the omelet comes fresh French bread and a glass of dry-but-fruity white wine that bubbles slightly. I wasn't hungry to begin with, but this food is so excellent, the more I eat the hungrier I get. The native watches me, pleased at my appetite.

"And what about the vial?" I ask, dabbing my lips with a heavy cloth napkin. "Is anyone here ailing? In need of medicine?" He doesn't understand, so I take out the vial and show it to him.

He pulls out the little stopple carefully and sniffs the contents. He smiles and nods, obviously knowing to which of V. Snerk's innumerable cousins (I assume innumerable, though today the town is deserted) the vial must go. I am about to ask him if he wouldn't mind giving it to the party in question for me, so I can be on my way. (The thought of going from door to door, knocking, asking, being directed from nameless person to nameless person, fatigues me. I don't mind doing V. a favor, but there's a limit. I have my own fish to fry.) In the next moment, however, the native has thrown back his turbaned head and drained the contents of the vial.

"Hey!" I shout, too late.

The native smiles, burps once, then shakes my hand warmly, as if thanking me. I conclude that by a great coincidence he himself is the party in question, although he seems perfectly healthy. But then, no one has said the stuff was medicine.

"What is it for?" I ask, curious.

"Gas," he says, but immediately I know he does not mean gas in the usual, terrestrial sense. Perhaps in McGulveyland some people have a condition that, if not treated, results in their sudden explosion. A buildup of visceral air. Who knows?

"By the way," I say, cleaning my bowl with the last piece of French bread, "do you have any bookstores in these parts?"

The native looks at me blankly.

"I mean," I pursue the question, "adult bookstores."

There is not a trace of a smile on his face. He is like a statue—uncomprehending or disapproving, I can't tell which. I change the subject.

6

Sherman had to do the midweek marketing. His mother couldn't carry all the groceries when she went on Saturday, because of her back, and anyway they always ran out of milk and bread and other things before the week was over. Limited space in the freezer. Or something might not be on sale that Saturday. Sherman had to cut coupons out of the papers and magazines, had to walk from aisle to aisle marking things off his list, clicking the red plastic calculator-counter in his left hand as he pushed a basket past toilet paper, bags of rice, or boxes of asparagus, and prayed nobody from school saw him. Mom yelled at him if he was careless about the prices. He had to figure out which was cheaper: $1.19 for six and a half ounces or .79 for four? Pennies here, pennies there, they added up. "I have two kids who will have to be put through college," Mom said. "That's eight years of tuition." Halves of ounces—or three for .89—made Sherman's mind cloud over every time, and the coupons, fifty cents off this versus a dollar-fifty off that, only thickened the cloud. Not to mention rebates and rain checks. He scowled from the effort of trying to keep his head straight, and secretly wished that once in a while the Potts family could treat itself. To ice-cream sandwiches, to root beer, and screw the pennies adding up. As if in punishment for this rebellious thought, who should he bump into at the end of the aisle but Susan and her mother, and in clear view of the sanitary napkins and tampons. He turned scarlet in a second; his face pounded. Susan said something about seeing him Friday at the dance, and her mother said something, too. Sherman didn't catch the mother's words, but could tell they weren't friendly. His appearance left a lot to be desired: he hadn't combed his hair, hadn't changed his shirt, and his shirt stank after a day at school. "It's time you started using deodorant," Mom had said. Because of the glands starting to percolate. Life would be a heap easier without glands starting to percolate.

7

The theory that Morgan first came up with, i.e., that some kind of space warp was scooping up complex organic molecules in objects that didn't move (in other words, food as opposed to trees or crops still in the ground, or people), struck us all as extremely stupid. Trees or radishes certainly didn't move much. Well, then, maybe motion wasn't what made the difference, Morgan said. Maybe it was the absence of electrical impulses, since there were electrical impulses in all living things.

He set up an apparatus that ran a weak current through an apple pie. The pie was sealed inside a box with a tiny window. It lasted a few days, but then disappeared. We caught the disappearance on film. One second the pie was there, the next it wasn't. Slowing down the film failed to show any transition state, any fading, or anything that would provide a clue to the process. So much for science.

The colony was faced with starvation. At the rate the food was disappearing, assuming the rate remained constant, we had about a month—two, tops, with the strictest rationing—before we became too weak to do anything and entered the downward spiral toward death, lying on our backs and watching the clouds sail by overhead.

I called a general meeting, not just an executive council, because the whole community had to be informed, and there were all sorts of wild rumors circulating anyway.

It was necessary to avoid a panic. To use our heads. As the people filed into the assembly hall, I nodded and smiled at them. I knew most of them by name. We had been through so much together. But now across our hope of a new life, of a better world, fell the shadow of a mortal threat.

"Citizens of New Batavia," I began, and in the hush that followed you could hear the crickets and the tree frogs, their soothing music, as if nothing evil could possibly occur in this peaceful paradise that we had found for ourselves, that we had risked all the perils of space to find. . . . "Something, we don't know what, is taking our food."

They chuckled, many of them, as if it were a joke. They knew, of course, that the food was vanishing, but didn't believe the problem was really serious: the Commander would solve the mystery, as he always did.

I realized then that we were not going to put our heads together. No, they were waiting for me—even the officers were waiting for me—to come up with the solution to the problem.

"Our supplies, Ned Bruckner tells me, are half gone," I went on, and had Ned stand up and confirm this. Ned was not too bright but as reliable as a cesium clock. "We have nothing to go on, no clues. So, until further notice, we must prepare ourselves for the worst." But the upturned faces in the hall were not grim. A few people were even smiling. When, I wondered, would the smiling stop? In a week? In a month?

"Rationing," I continued, "effective immediately. We cut our daily intake by half. Half-portions of everything. In other words, half a bowl of cereal in the morning. One cup of coffee if you usually have two. And that goes for cookies, also," I said, eyeing little Billy LoBianco, who was famous for his sweet tooth. The freckled kid giggled, showing his missing front teeth, and the audience laughed. "Secondly, shorten the time, as much as possible, between the harvesting and the eating. Whatever has been taking our food doesn't act immediately—or at least not yet. As long as a potato is in the ground, or a berry is on the vine, or a squeak-fish is in the water, it's safe."

"Next thing, you'll tell us we have to eat our food live, on the hoof," quipped Barkley, and the audience laughed again. The only "cattle" on the planet was the dinker, a kind of gerbil that had tiny gray scales instead of fur, no ears, and a funny trumpetlike snout. The animal was prolific, slow, and tripped a lot when it tried to flee ("No natural enemies," sniffed Poindexter, "or it wouldn't have lasted"), which made it ridiculously easy to catch. But you would need several dozen dinkers to make a single serving of stew. The thought of trying to eat the animals live and kicking was grotesque.

"We need to develop strategies to minimize food storage," I said. "I'll put Buster in charge of that. Go to him if you have suggestions." Buster rose and waved, corncob pipe in his mouth, and there was applause. "And in the meantime," I concluded, "Havilland, Pliscou, and I will see if we can get the subcom working and call the Guild for help."

That took some of the lightness out of the proceedings. When the subcom broke down six months ago, a deadserious delegation approached me—Cuthbertson at its head—with the request that it not be fixed.

"You want to burn our bridges behind us, eh?" I said then, squinting at them.

"There's nothing here, Commander, that we can't handle," Jack replied.

Secretly I agreed with him. Still, it had made me uneasy not to have the subcom in working order. It meant one less option, and you never knew what the future had in store.

The subcom was a sort of symbolic umbilical cord—I understood that—and the colonists wanted it severed. Certainly, if you went to a desert island to get away from it all, you wouldn't be happy to find a telephone, connected, and a telephone book in your palm-tree house. But what if one summer evening you came down with appendicitis?

Now, I thought, our survival depended on repairing— and swiftly—that subetheric wireless gathering dust in Havilland's toolshed.

Would we be able to do it? And if we did, would the Guild be able to help us? The enemy—or plague, or warp—was invisible, invisible to the eye and to all our instruments, like a ghost, or like a supernatural curse cast by an ancient race hidden in the bowels of the planet and seething with hatred for the human intruders. Perhaps the giant emeralds carried that curse. . . . No, I told myself, that was nonsense.

After the meeting, at home, I reached in the hutch for the bona fide Terran Scotch to pour myself a double shot, because I needed to steady my nerves, but the bottle was empty. Bone dry.

8

I find an adult bookstore in a cave in a mountainous polar region. Definitely off the beaten path. My fingers are so numb that when I try to browse, I can't turn the pages at first. The owner, a bear, growls at me, because in my haste to get to the pornography I forgot to take off my snowshoes and tracked in quite a bit of snow. I apologize, blushing, even though this is McGulveyland, not reality, so there's no need to blush, the bear isn't going to tell anybody who knows me in Penn Hills. Hurriedly I check my snowshoes at the entrance to the cave, propping them against a rock.

Unfortunately, none of the books are suitable, they're all about spanking and being spanked, which doesn't turn me on at all, and people urinating on people, which I find stupid. This, in other words, is a specialty adult bookstore, only for perverts. It can't do much business, surely, in this wilderness.

But even if I found a suitable book here, I would have a problem paying for it. The owner: I doubt that he will accept currency, coin. The way he follows me with his eyes, as I browse, gives me the willies. When he grimaces, his mouth half-open, in contempt (probably because I'm not buying anything), you can see two rows of large, sharp teeth. I imagine the only tender he will accept is raw red meat, and all I have on me, for this trek through the tundra, is a tasteless twist of pemmican.

9

Dave picked him up at a quarter to seven, which barely gave him time to get dressed after clearing the table, putting away the food, washing the dishes, changing the water in Terhune's bowl, and reading Priscilla the Pill the riot act on what to do and what not to do—with the emergency phone numbers by the phone—until Mom came home at eleven, since Mom was taking that accounting course now on Tuesday and Friday nights. Priscilla the Pill had ignored him, of course, as she always did. Her eyes got glassy whenever he talked directly into her face.

Maybe he would be lucky, and she would use the stove, which she wasn't supposed to do when she was alone in the house, to make herself hot chocolate, and accidentally get her stupid blue teddy-bear nightgown in the fire and be burnt to a crisp, with no one around to hear her stupid little screams of pain. Sherman, cursing, gave his hair a mad, last-ditch combing when Dave honked outside in the driveway—his hair was an even greater embarrassment than the red-hot eruption at the corner of his mouth, his hair was the hair of a Sesame Street puppet—then he banged out of the house, breathless, but remembered to bolt the door, because Mom would have fifty conniptions if the door wasn't bolted when she came home. Dave, grinning, smoking a cigarette, steered with his right wrist instead of his hands, resting the wrist on top of the wheel, as if he weren't driving a car but sitting in an easy chair and half-dozing through a no-hitter or a golf tournament on Sunday afternoon television. Sherman was so nervous, with a stomach full of spaghetti eaten too fast, that he felt very close to throwing up. Wouldn't that be awful, he thought, to vomit red spaghetti all over Susan's new taffeta in the middle of the spring dance?

10

It's in an Asian-type bazaar, finally, that I stumble upon a sex book. It was under some old pots and pans in the corner of the shop, a mildewed paperback limp and grimy from the thumbing of several hundred (at least) sweating adolescents. You know right away that it will suit the purpose. The title is *Lust Kittens*, and on the cover is a redhead with her blouse three-quarters open and her jaw slack, as if someone just bopped her over the head with a large wooden mallet. Hands trembling, I open the book at random and find people having an orgasm. Excellent, excellent.

But the owner is returning from the back room, drawing aside the Oriental bead curtain, so hastily I stuff the book into my hip pocket and stand up, pretending to be interested in an eggbeater—because this is a shop for kitchen utensils, not pornography.

"Found something you like?" the merchant asks cheerfully. He is wearing a fez and has a mustache.

"Er, yes," I say, awkwardly holding the eggbeater. "For Mother's Day."

"Ah," he says, giving me (I think) a strange look.

And that's all he says, so after a painful silence I ask: "How much?"

"Three thousand rupees," he says smoothly, not batting an eye.

"How much would that be in dollars?" I'm getting weak in the knees. I have no idea what the exchange rate is in McGulveyland. This is my first purchase.

"$15.95."

To me this seems a bit steep for an eggbeater, and I wonder if money spent in McGulveyland will reduce my wallet on Earth. If one pays five dollars for something in a dream, one doesn't expect to wake up five dollars poorer. On the other hand, McGulveyland isn't exactly a dream.

I stand, holding the eggbeater, undecided. The merchant in the fez does not suggest a lower price. He watches me with a bland face. Perhaps, I think, this is really a pornography shop, not a kitchen-utensil shop, and he's really charging me for the dirty paperback that he knows (somehow) I stuffed into my hip pocket when he wasn't looking.

Even so, $15.95 is just too much. I can't afford it,

having no job of my own yet, like Dave; my allowance is so small that at the end of the week there's only a little change, fifty cents maybe, no more. (If I ask Mom for more of an allowance, I'll get a shrill lecture on the sacrifices she's made and the sacrifices I should make, and the lecture will continue, off and on, for a month.)

I start to put the eggbeater back in the basket of eggbeaters, wondering if I have the nerve to attempt a theft, a shoplifting, by leaving the premises now, careful not to turn my back to the merchant, because a few inches of the book must show. Would he call the police? Worse, would he complain to Mr. McGulvey?

"Make it five," I say.

"Five what?" he asks.

"Dollars."

He sighs, looks at the ceiling, shrugs. "It's highway robbery, but all right. You're too much for me, young man. I have twelve mouths to feed, but no matter, no matter." And he takes the five dollars as they're counted out, one by one, into his palm.

The eggbeater, when I look at it more closely in the street, where the light is better, turns out to be a piece of junk, more a toy than an eggbeater, all flimsy tin, not steel or aluminum. It would be worth, maybe, a quarter, a dime, to a little girl who wanted to play house. I toss it into the gutter.

But the book . . . At the thought of smuggling *Lust Kittens* into Mr. McGulvey's magic library, my blood begins to pound, my mouth gets dry. Jesus, what an adventure this will make. I can't wait.

Chapter Three

• 1 •

We held a council of war, Sir Frank, Sir Phil, Sir Mike, Sir Gardyloo, and I, sitting grimly around the downstairs table in our firehouse, only five of us now and all beginning to cough yellow fumes. Clearly, time was on the side of the enemy: if we didn't defeat the dragons soon, we'd find ourselves in the Cuspidor City Hospital with liver damage or worse.

"We're getting nowhere," said Sir Frank. "The dragons outnumber us, and we haven't made a dent in their operations. It's almost like we're providing them with entertainment."

I couldn't help thinking that Sir Frank, so far, hadn't killed a single dragon. All he seemed to do in battle was trapeze tricks. An uncharitable thought.

"How are the other companies of knights faring?" asked Sir Gardyloo.

"No better," said Sir Frank. "Worse."

"We have to come up with a different strategy," Sir Mike put in, always rational.

"Well," I said, "they spy on us. Let's spy on them. Infiltrate."

"What are you talking about?" said Sir Phil. "How can we infiltrate?"

"We disguise ourselves as dragons."

63

Sir Frank made a face and rolled his eyes up, as if he had never heard anything so stupid.

"No, wait, I think he has something there," said Sir Mike, and a discussion followed. If they could disguise themselves as us, Sir Mike argued, then we should be able to disguise ourselves as them. All that was needed was green construction paper, tagboard, and perhaps a small, concealed blowtorch to simulate fire-breathing.

Sir Gardyloo objected that the paper and tagboard would be flammable. Papier-mâché? That would be flammable, too. And plastic? Plastic would melt.

Sheets of asbestos, Sir Phil ventured, might do, but asbestos did not come in colors, as far as he knew, and if we painted the asbestos green, the asbestos might be fire-resistant but the paint wouldn't be.

Sir Mike pointed out, impatient, that dragons didn't breathe fire on one another. If we were just careful using the blowtorches, there should be no problem.

"And what about their language?" Sir Gardyloo asked. "We have no guarantee that they speak English among themselves. Why should they? They're a different species, they probably originated in a different solar system. The odds of them speaking English are pretty slim, if you ask me."

Sir Mike nodded slowly, his brow knit. A good point.

Sir Frank turned to me then and said: "It's your idea, Sir Sherm. You do it if you want to, though I wouldn't advise it. The scheme seems harebrained to me. We face danger enough without sticking our heads in the lion's mouth."

I looked at my fellow knights. Sir Mike was game; he would go along for the ride if I asked him. But Sir Frank was probably right that such a sortie was suicidal. On the other hand, what else could we do? This was a lost war.

The dragons outclassed us. Our defense of the city was a joke. "What the hell," I thought. "Faint heart never won fair damsel. If I get killed in this adventure, I get killed. It wouldn't be the first time. And if that happens, then good riddance to the adventure. This one certainly hasn't been a winner."

"I'll do it," I said, feeling a thrill of heroism. They all looked at me with a new respect.

2

And as Sergeant Sherm I came to pretty much the same conclusion. The psi-fiend had gone into high gear: two senators had been shot while jogging, a Cabinet member had been knifed at a luncheon, there was a flood of hate mail—or hate telegrams—at the White House, and several syndicated columnists were advocating martial law, the nuking into submission of various stubborn nations, trade embargoes, a return to the gold standard, and the clubbing of baby seals. I had never seen such hysteria in the media. *The Washington Post* ran headlines so large and shrill, it looked like an oversize tabloid. The talk shows on the radio were filled with four-letter words and statements so defamatory, I couldn't believe my ears.

"A few more days of this," I told Borgenicht at his cousin's garden apartment in Gaithersburg, where on my advice he was holing up (because the aura of a fifth-level adept, no matter how carefully shielded, would bring the psi-fiend like a bee to honey, and I didn't need the aggravation, on top of everything else, of having to battle a rearranged old friend), "a few more days of this, and the U.S. of A. goes down the tube."

"But what can we do?" said Borgenicht, throwing up his

hands. The strain of recent events had made him completely gray.

Of course, I could throw in the towel and return to my mist-enshrouded castle at Loch Shin, hoping that this extradimensional menace would be satisfied with its conquest of America. That, engorged on the Constitution, the Bill of Rights, Four Score and Seven Years Ago, E Pluribus Unum, and the Almighty Dollar, it would leave Europe alone, losing interest in the rest of our planet. There is wisdom in knowing when to get the hell out.

But history teaches us—does it not?—that geopolitical appetites are never satisfied.

"The beast is too powerful," muttered Borgenicht, shaking his head.

"I've decided to enter its home dimension," I said.

The old inspector looked at me uncomprehendingly.

"It's the only way," I went on. "One to one, I am no match for the thing. At best, I can defend myself—just barely. Or foil it for the briefest moment only. Nor would it be right for us to call in my illustrious mentor Hsün Hsien Wu Chang, even in an advisory capacity. He has paid his dues."

"I do not understand this allusion to dues," said Borgenicht.

"No matter."

"Surely, if the very nation hangs in the balance . . ."

"The only way to learn the psi-fiend's weakness, dear Borgy, for each creature has its weakness, is to visit its world of origin."

"You are mad!"

"Its world of origin, I know, will not be hospitable."

"There may be beings there far more powerful, and far more malevolent, than it!"

"Quite. And yet I must take that chance."

"You are mad!"

How often had I heard those words before.

With a rueful-wry smile on my lips, I whisked myself, on a lilac-scented gust summoned from the Mystic Grove of Night, up to the great Compass Rose of Planes, where all worlds meet, real and unreal—all save Ykranórsl—at the House of Doors. There, among endless marble arches, columns, and galleries, I tracked the spoor of the psifiend, a thing not at all difficult to do, since the beast had plowed through without any respect for the formalities and amenities, making tatters of various greeting/introduction/privacy spells in different languages and magics. I could have found the door to its dimension with my eyes closed, just following my nose.

The door, obsidian, trembled, as from tremendous volcanic activity far away. I gripped my hidden amulet, the five-cent turtle that no one knew of, and with a whispered incantation projected myself through, astral body and all, into a colorless hurricane.

3

A lot of heavy breathing, long moans, and whimpers of ecstasy. It worked, damn it, it worked. Hurray! Señor Sherm is so excited he can't see straight; the sultry Italian beauty recumbent on the purple crewelwork settee is a blur before him, as if he were in a Turkish bath or underwater with twisting ribbons of pale pink champagne bubbles streaming past; but he knows her mouth is open, her jaw jutted, and her eyes half-rolled back as the gauzelike excuse for clothing—lacy blouse, flimsy, clinging skirt—is waiting, begging him to remove it now, to tear it away from those splendid swollen breasts and maddeningly curved, rocking hips. Señor Sherm's heart is thump-thumping with such violence, it's as if he's gripped a jackhammer and can't let go or is on a snorting bronco that's broken the neck of every rider, even those flinty, dry cowpokes who can roll their own with just the left hand while the right holds the reins. His hands, shaking terribly, are taking forever to unbutton, unsnap, pull down, pull off, and I'm beginning to fear he won't make it, he's so excited, it's his first time, after all, so I whisper in his ear, "Hold back, man, hold back, damn it! Take a deep breath! Count to ten!" But how can he take a deep breath—the poor bastard can hardly breathe, he's breathing so hard—Christ, I hope he doesn't pass out on me, because the Italian beauty now is groaning so loud and urgently and throatily from her need, from her hunger, that the groaning is practically a wail, a full scream, please take me oh please oh, and the beat increases doubles, quadruples, goes berserk like bongo drums in a Burmese opium den at midnight when there's heat lightning and no moon. Señor Sherm, all thumbs, gasping like a fish out of water, struggles frantically with his stubborn zipper.

4

Cory got it working. "Come on over, Commander," he said on the phone.

On the way to Havilland's place I passed our silver ship. It stood tall and proud upon its great fins, still vibrant with power, it seemed, though the hull was little more than an empty shell now, since we had cannibalized most of its machinery in setting up the colony. A regret—a brief flicker of regret—stirred within me: for that earlier time of danger and hope, when the planet, the fourth from

Lambda Eridani, first hove into view on our screens, a beautiful blue-green marble gleaming against the velvet black of space.

It was the action I missed. Action is a terrific tonic—but unfortunately habit-forming, which makes a man restless when he has to go over lists of things, or sit at meetings and hear complaints about food supplies and rationing, or copter over to the pumping facility at North End because another squeak-fish got through the filter somehow and ruined one of the transformers, an expensive piece of equipment that Scrig has no idea how to replace. No idea, because he isn't using his head.

I picked my way carefully over the huge roots of the tree growing in the middle of Havilland's living room and found him, Cory, and Morgan in the kitchen, all bending over the subcom on the kitchen table. The thing was plugged in and humming.

"Good work," I said, and they blushed with pleasure.

There was hardly any static. They had somebody named Rallston on the line, and his voice was so clear, it didn't even need to be redigitalized. Amazing technology: the guy was ten parsecs away, but he could have been next door, and this miracle was made possible by an apparatus that weighed no more than a toaster and ran on regular household current.

"They tell me you have a problem," said Rallston when I put on the earphones and introduced myself. "What is it, Commander, not enough women for you out there in the boondocks?"

Typical Guild humor.

I explained the situation, feeling like an idiot. I tried to be factual, specific, but inwardly groaned—listening to myself talk—at how stupid it sounded. Disappearing food? I pictured Rallston nodding, smiling painfully, waiting for me to get to the punch line—an awful pun, probably—of this protracted, unbelievably inane joke.

But instead, when I finished, he said, with unexpected seriousness: "You people have been out of touch for a while, haven't you?"

"About six months," I said.

"Yes, I know. Turning your backs on civilization, not reading the papers. It's typical for a young colony."

I felt a chill. "What's been going on?" I asked.

"The same thing."

"What do you mean?"

"The same thing that's been going on at your New Batavia."

It took me a moment to digest that. "Are you telling me," I asked, "that food has been disappearing other places?"

There was a pause at the other end. "Not just other places, Commander," Rallston finally said. "It's everywhere."

"What do you mean, everywhere?" The chill grew inside me.

"Everywhere. The galaxy. The whole damn universe, as far as we know."

"How . . . how is that possible?"

"Good question."

5

It was uncomfortable, itchy, inside my disguise of green construction paper and tagboard, and the blowtorch, held under my left arm, dug into my armpit, which made the arm numb and the fingers tingle. But the dragons didn't seem to notice anything wrong—perhaps because of my smell, which was a good touch provided by Sir Mike. He figured that the noxious creatures would "perfume" them-

selves accordingly. "Eau de sewer," he had said, anointing
me with a jarful of sludge taken from some old plumbing
in some old cellar. "You'll be one of the boys."

The dragon nest I infiltrated was in a suite at the finest
hotel in Cuspidor. Practically an entire floor. They must
have had loads of money. (But we suspected as much.)
They sat around, not doing anything, perhaps waiting to
go on a raid, so I sat around, too. They puffed on vile
cigars (it was all I could do to keep from coughing), and
occasionally exchanged a few words in a foreign language.
Now and then I discharged a little flame from my blowtorch, as if yawning, careful of course not to ignite my
disguise. Hours passed.

Then the phone rang. One of the dragons picked up the
receiver, listened, and turned to the rest of us and said:
"Nel mezzo del cammin!" And everyone replied, with
apparent pleasure, "Nel mezzo del cammin!" and jumped
up and made for the door or, if they felt like flying, the
window. The raid had been chosen. I ran out also, but in
the hall a dragon put its head close to mine and said: "Mi
ritrovai per una selva oscura che la diritta via era smarrita."
I nodded and muttered, "Era smarrita," and that seemed
to satisfy it. (I thought, "Whew!")

We got into black limousines. In the limousine I was in,
a dragon gave instructions. I nodded and nodded, pretending to understand. A map was passed around. With a
gasp I recognized our fire station in the center, circled.
Our company was the target this time! How could I alert
my comrades, and without betraying myself? The dragon
leader handed me a box with a plunger, the kind used to
detonate dynamite, and said: "Nessun maggior dolore." I
nodded, but nodding, now, wasn't good enough; the dragon
expected an answer. "Dolore," I mumbled. But the dragon
shook its head and said, right in my face: "Che ricordarsi

del tempo felice! Nella miseria! E quindi uscimmo a riveder le stelle!" I thought, "The jig is up," but then we arrived at our destination and everyone poured out of the limousine, so I didn't have to answer.

Out on the pavement, we stormed the firehouse, using both the front and back entrances. I figured I would duck into a side room, get rid of this stupid costume, and join my fellow knights in the fight. But Sir Gardyloo leaped out from behind a cupboard with his sword drawn. He would have run me through, too, if I hadn't parried quickly with the box-and-plunger.

His face became strange—browner, fatter. Steam shot from his ears and nostrils. I looked down and saw that the plunger was depressed. What had I done? Then I knew: it was a microwave device that the dragons had given me, and I had microwaved my old buddy to death—and after we had shared an adventure (a much better adventure than this one) on the planet Saraband. I had cooked him, cooked him from the center out!

As Sir Gardyloo fell, the sword slipping from his boiled hand, a dragon's head appeared in the window and, laughing, said: "Conosco i segni dell'antica fiamma."

It all became clear to me: they had set me up, they had set this whole thing up. They knew from the first that I was no dragon, and they had been laughing at me the whole time, while I pretended to yawn with my blowtorch and sat carefully on the sofa, in their suite, afraid of putting a crease in my green construction paper. Ah, what a fool I was! And how wicked they!

6

Mr. McGulvey invites me to go fishing with him about a week after my return. It's only when we're out on the lake—a quiet morning—that I notice that there's no hook at the end of his line. Also: no can of bait beside him or at his feet in the boat. How are we supposed to catch fish without worms? But I don't ask, I wait and see, reminding myself that this is McGulveyland. As I watch, he ties a knot in his line, then makes a loose loop, a kind of noose, and for a moment I think: "What, are we going to *hang* the fish?" But he doesn't stop there; he makes another loop farther up on the line, then connects the two loops with a third loop, in a complicated way that I can't follow. His large fingers work the string patiently, while the tip of his tongue shows between his teeth and sometimes rests against his upper lip. Now I begin to wonder. Did we come out here, in the middle of the lake, to tie knots? I sigh. I guess I'm not in the right spirit this morning.

What Mr. McGulvey has made is a kind of cradle—not the string game of cat's cradle, but a halter or harness for the fish to swim into. I can't imagine any fish being that obliging: it would have to put one fin here, one fin there, and its tail so . . . and this without any food, real or fake, offered in payment. But I say nothing.

Time passes slowly on the lake. The water, slate gray, has hardly any ripples in it, and mist blurs the wooded hills around us. The sun won't be up for another hour, and you get the feeling that most things are still sound asleep. The ideal time for a fisherman, I suppose, but I find it boring.

Unless . . . Did Mr. McGulvey take me out here for a man-to-man talk? About my sneaking *Lust Kittens* into his

magic library, dropping it into that little dusty place behind the walnut credenza while he was out by the mailbox
yesterday talking to Old Corduroy (which usually takes a
long time, although they don't ever seem to say much)? I
search his face while he prepares his fish cradle, but
detect no cloud, no trace of displeasure. He doesn't know.
I'm in the clear.

"Now," says Mr. McGulvey with a smile, finished, "you
do yours. I'll help you."

He is not a good teacher, or else I've suddenly become
unusually obtuse and clumsy. I loop to the left instead of
to the right, or tuck the string under instead of over. This
reminds me of the awful time I had in Cub Scouts, when
Mom became, briefly, a den mother and made us all do
lanyards. My confusion finally infects Mr. McGulvey, so
that he, teaching, himself forgets how to tie a fish cradle
and has to keep checking the first one, counting its loops
and muttering "left . . . right . . . left . . ." I begin to
think we'll be doing this all day, especially when he wor-
ries, under his breath, that maybe the first one wasn't
done right, he isn't sure, the thing has to be completely
right or it won't work, and so on. But then, unexpectedly,
my fish cradle is finished, and then we're both fishing, he
off one side of the boat and I off the other.

I'm not that surprised when we start catching fish. What
surprises me is that the fish cradle hauls not only a fish out
of the lake but also a sizable bubble of water with it. It's
like pulling up a fish inside a fishbowl, except there's no
bowl, just this clever network of string that enables the
fish to swim around peacefully while you raise it to eye
level.

"It's surface tension that does it," Mr. McGulvey explains.

Now I understand why the fish are so obliging. Going
fishing is as much an activity for them as it is for us: while

we look at them, they look at us and at our world. It must get tedious being in a lake all the time, where nothing happens. When we're all, we and the fish, done looking, Mr. McGulvey and I return them to the water and pick up new ones.

They're lovely, I have to admit, even though I'm not exactly in a poetic mood this morning. The fish are all the colors of the rainbow—and when the sun finally rises, filling the sky with pinks and yellows, and the lake catches all that, the very air around us seems to become a mirror for the fish. I would thank Mr. McGulvey for this rare experience but can't find the words.

No, that's not true: I know the words, all right, I just don't feel clean enough to say them.

7

Time slowed to such a crawl in the classroom that the second hand on the wall clock over Mrs. Decowski's gray head seemed to have to make an effort each time to click to the next second mark. And there was an entire month of this stifling imprisonment to go, though the air outside already smelled of summer fields, dandelions, milkweed. And after that month, Sherman had two years to go, another two stretches in the penitentiary of education, before he graduated. Two years of having to sit still from September to June and listen to a droning voice and smell chalk dust and look for the millionth time at the same stupid graffiti on his desk. Mrs. Decowski called on Bob about adverbial phrases, which Bob got through the same way he played basketball in gym—flat-footed and double-dribbling, which Mr. Hollis, out of charity, never blew his whistle over. Mrs. Decowski, too, went easy on Bob.

Barbara was next, and of course she knew all about adverbs, holding her mouth the way Priscilla the Pill did when she had a secret and wasn't going to tell. As Dave was called on and said matter-of-factly, coolly, casually, that he hadn't done his homework, Sherman phased to the psi-fiend's home dimension, but didn't have time to accomplish anything there, because Mrs. Decowski called on him next, and although he hadn't done his homework either, he wasn't able, quickly phasing back to English 10, to say that matter-of-factly, coolly, or casually. If Mrs. Decowski went easy on Bob, she didn't understand—or didn't like—Sherman's trouble getting past certain letters of the alphabet. It made her impatient, and she was annoyed anyway, now, having two students back-to-back who hadn't done their adverb homework. In her steel voice she told Sherman to go to the blackboard. Sherman, seeing this command to stand up coming, and despite his clenched teeth, developed, as he sat, a complete erection in less than three seconds. With everyone's eyes on him, he turned scarlet. Desperate, to stall for time, he dropped his notebook, murmured, "One minute," and bent over, groping for it on the floor, praying with all his soul either to be saved by the bell or for his erection to go away—now oh please now—but the bell wouldn't ring for another five minutes at least, and Sherman, very soon, would have to get up out of his seat, orders were orders, and go to the blackboard in front of the class. And he knew that the erection demon, like the stutter demon, never showed mercy and in fact seemed to take pleasure turning a boy's worst nightmares of humiliation into horrible reality.

8

Professor Sherm first noticed something wrong when, in the morning paper at breakfast, he read that the Pirates defeated the Yankees 9–2 to pull into first place with only a week to go now before the World Series, and that Pittsburgh fans were going bananas because the Pirates had not made it to a World Series since 1932.

Chewing thoughtfully on a piece of English muffin, he put the paper down and hmmed. The Pirates had been in a World Series in 1971 and 1979, against the Orioles both times, and won the pennant both times, and they had also won the 1960 World Series against the Yankees. Moreover, the Pirates couldn't possibly play the Yankees *before* a World Series, since they were and had always been in the National League, while the Yankees were . . .

"Either this article is a prank," said Professor Sherm, "or someone has been tampering with the time lines again."

The time lines had been tampered with as recently as last year, over the Christmas vacation. A disgruntled student (why were students always disgruntled?) had broken into the Higher Physics Laboratory in Building C, a top-secret installation run jointly by the university and the government, and attempted to alter the past, using the Chronotron so that he wouldn't flunk—or, rather, wouldn't have flunked—his Organic Chemistry 327 course the year before, since that was the one thing on his record keeping him out of medical school. He claimed afterward, in his defense, that his father would kill him if he didn't become a doctor. Apparently there had been nothing but doctors in the family for seven generations.

The student, however, didn't warm up the machine properly and didn't pay attention to the retrotemporal differentials on the scanoscope, with the result that instead of changing his Organic Chemistry 327 grade of the previous year he fouled up some Etruscan dynasty successions, and it took the experts—physicists and historians—almost two weeks to put everything back where it belonged. Not to mention the apologies that had to be made to several indignant foreign heads of state. (For example, three words had disappeared from the "Marseillaise." Yes, the tangled branchings of cause and effect through time were far-reaching and difficult to sort out, a veritable mare's nest of fishing-line snarls.)

Sherm was one of that team of experts who served, in such emergencies, as Guardians of Time. He was a historian from Harvard and had a mind—his colleagues all said—like a steel trap. He was the kind of man who happened to know the "Marseillaise" by heart and that the Pirates had not been in a World Series in the 1930s, the 1940s, or the 1950s.

"We are putting you on probation," Dean Fix had told the disgruntled student, shaking an admonitory finger, "for unauthorized and irresponsible tinkering with the Continuum."

And then there was the time that sophomore coed from Tennessee—a sweet-looking thing, with her snub nose and cute hillbilly accent (who would have thought her capable of such a crime?)—had climbed through an unlocked window one night, got to the Chronotron, and did away with her boyfriend, because he had told her he loved someone else. (A flick of a switch, a turn of a dial, and—poof!—you did not exist, because the boat your great-grandparents came over on in 1919, for example, sprung a leak before it reached Ellis Island.)

By coincidence her tampering with the time lines did away, in addition to her boyfriend, with Dean Fix himself, and he expelled her as soon as the experts reconstituted him. Sherm never saw the man so angry. The dean could hardly speak; he actually foamed at the mouth.

Finishing the English muffin, Sherm put on his corduroy sports jacket with the suede elbow patches, filled his pipe with his favorite blend of latakia, tucked the newspaper under his arm, and set out across the carpetlike lawn of the campus to Building C.

Little did the world know what mighty matters of moment had been decided behind these sleepy, ivy-covered walls. The Chronotron, since its invention in 1981, had already saved the world two times. Sherm remembered the April night he received that hysterical phone call from Carl Hofstadter, president of the university . . .

[FLASHBACK]

"Sherm! We need your help! I hope to God you can help us!"

"What seems to be the problem, Carl?"

"The missiles are on their way! Soviet missiles! The Strategic Air Command just informed me!"

"Carl, please, I can hear you. You don't have to shout."

"They—our side has pushed the button, too! It's finally happened! I can't believe it! I thought we could live in peace, work something out, coexist! Christ! We have eleven minutes! Eleven minutes, Sherm! Eleven minutes, and it's bye-bye-kerplooey for the whole human race! And Bertha and I were going to take a vacation next month, to the Berkshires—"

[END OF FLASHBACK]

. . . and remembered how he ran out of the house in his pajamas, barefoot, and got to the Chronotron in the nick of time, sprinting, just before the bombs fell, and how he set everything back a day, and fiddled with a factor here, a factor there. Nobody knew, now, except him and a handful of time experts, that the capital of Russia used to be Ladograd, not Moscow, and that the composer of *Prince Igor* had been, before the adjustment, Count Kulyshnikov-Kropotovski instead of the chemist Borodin.

9

Princess Martha Anne, wrapped in a gray cloak, attended Sir Gardyloo's funeral, taking time out from her own adventure, whatever that was. A moving gesture, this, particularly since she was nobility and Sir Gardyloo had been just another kid—and from the lower middle class. You could tell he was from the lower middle class by the language he used, his stubby fingers, and his button nose. His fingers and nose were six feet under now, with the rest of him, food for worms. That was the fate of all of us, I reflected sadly, whether we came from a storybook castle or Chicago.

The princess was here at the cemetery for old times' sake. Hadn't we fought, the three of us side by side, the hideous warted Frops on the battlements of Zin? Though she had done most of the fighting. Of course, they had trained her for that. But Sir Gardyloo (R.I.P.) and I pitched in at crucial moments, taking turns saving the day. (The Frops had seven arms apiece and eyes on the sides and in the back of their heads, so you really had to be on your toes.) Sir Gardyloo was clumsy but consistently lucky; villains, typically, would trip just before getting into posi-

tion to brain him or blow him to smithereens. But now his
luck had run out and he was cooked. Cooked by my hand.

Did my fellow knights hold that against me? Did Princess Martha Anne? I couldn't tell. We all had our heads
bowed as the Cuspidor minister went on in a singsong
about the Heavenly Kingdom. Sir Phil was wearing a
mask, for his asthma; on him it looked like a feed bag. Sir
Mike's expression, what I could see of it, was pained. Sir
Frank was impassive, as if waiting patiently, stoically, for
something unpleasant, like an injection.

On our way out, at the gate, a voice whispered: "As you
sow, so shall you reap." I looked around. No one was
near. A ventriloquist? And what was the message supposed to mean? A warning? I repeated the words to myself. Not a comfortable sentence: too many *s*'s.

10

At Building C, Professor Sherm had to show his ID to
all three guards in turn—the one at the gate, the one at
the door, and the one at the desk—even though they had
known him for years and all worshiped him. Security was
security, and the Chronotron was even more top secret
than biological warfare.

Arnie MacTavish, a red-goateed experimental physics
professor who played tennis with Sherm at the faculty
courts and never minded losing, waved Sherm over impa-
tiently with a hairy arm. He wanted to show him something in the lab. "I need your opinion on this," he said as
he walked down the hall, in such a hurry that Sherm
almost had to trot to keep up. Arnie barreled through the
swinging doors that said KEEP OUT: AUTHORIZED PERSONNEL
ONLY, and he led Sherm to a bench piled high with Bun-

sen burners, Tesla coils, and Van de Graaff generators. "Here," he said, pointing to a graph on a strip of computer paper, "and here," showing Sherm a page packed with calculations. He stabbed an angry, hairy finger at the equation that said h equaled 6.625×10^{-28} erg second.

"Arnie," said Sherm, "you know this is Greek to me."

"It's Planck's constant."

"And what if it is, old friend?"

"Then we're in big trouble, Sherm."

"Wait a minute. Are you telling me that this constant . . . is wrong?"

Arnie nodded, paced, swung his arms like an old sea bird trying to get into the air but not succeeding. He knocked over an Erlenmeyer flask with his sleeve, but paid no attention to that, though the brown liquid that spilled on the floor bubbled and smoked. "Planck's constant," he said, tugging on his red goatee, "is one of the fundamental constants of the universe, like π or the speed of light."

Sherm felt a chill. "How much is it off by?"

"A factor of ten."

Sherm whistled. This was no amateurish tinkering with the Continuum, no mere sneaking of the Pirates into the American League, this was full-blown sabotage and it struck at the very warp and woof of reality. "We better call a meeting of the Guardians of Time," he said.

Arnie blinked. "The what?"

"The Guardians of Time."

"What Guardians of Time?"

That was when Professor Sherm realized the full extent of the emergency. Without another word he ran—every second was precious—to the control room where the scanoscope was and the three-foot-thick molybdenum glass window providing a view of the enormous Chronotron that shimmered around the clock with Cherenkov radiation like a fluorescent ghost in an uninhabited gymnasium.

But the sign on the control room door said not DO NOT ENTER: HIGH VOLTAGE, as it was supposed to, but MEN, and when Sherm rushed in, he found not the familiar yet always awe-inspiring banks of dials and flickering lights and number-filled monitor screens, but a row of urinals. Opposite the urinals was a row of stalls. His mouth fell open, his pipe clattered on the tiled floor and broke into two pieces.

Behind him, Arnie said: "Sherm, are you feeling all right?"

Sherm turned slowly to the physicist and looked into his eyes. "Arnie," he said in a strangely calm voice that echoed ominously in the empty men's room, "it's up to you and me now. Fortunately I have a photographic memory and once happened to see all the blueprints, and what I don't know you'll be able to figure out. . . ."

"What in hell are you talking about?"

"The Chronotron, Arnie—we have to rebuild it. We have to rebuild everything. We may be too late, yes, but we have to try, try until the last moment, to keep the fabric from unraveling."

Arnie MacTavish regarded his colleague with the mixture of horror and compassion one feels for great minds that have finally plunged into madness. "Perhaps . . . perhaps you should take a vacation," he suggested gently. "All work and no play . . . Your social life has been neglected. . . ."

But Sherm was walking quickly back through the lab, and Arnie had to trot to keep up with him. Trotting, the physicist noticed—although he thought nothing of it at the time, because of his agitation about Planck's constant and now his friend's inexplicable behavior—paw prints on the floor. The paw prints led out of the men's room and meandered from work station to work station. They were catlike, though too large, by a factor of five or six, for a cat.

"I'll call Hofstadter," Sherm was thinking out loud. "If he still exists, that is. Let's keep our fingers crossed. He'll be able to get us the funding, the equipment . . . But, of course, we'll have to adjust our specs for the new constants, whatever they are . . . It won't be easy . . . As long as we can keep the fabric from unraveling."

"What fabric is that?" asked Arnie.

Sherm stopped, looked straight at him, then said gravely: "*The* fabric, old friend. The original fabric. The fabric underlying all fabrics."

11

But first they had to pick up Dave's date, Mary. She wasn't ready, because of her dress and her hair. Dave came down the steps and told Sherman he would wait in the Donaldsons' living room but Sherman should stay in the car. Sherman counted minutes on his wristwatch and looked at the silhouettes of the maple trees against the early evening sky. They were going to be late; it was already seven; at this rate they wouldn't get to the dance until 7:45. Sherman let the second hand make two whole circuits, then in desperation phased to the psi-fiend's home dimension, to the

12

colorless hurricane

13

but couldn't concentrate, because now it was more than
five after and still no Dave appeared in the doorway with
his date. Sherman chewed on his knuckles. Why did he
always have to be so nervous, so high-strung, his heart
going like the heart of a Chihuahua in the summer? At this
rate he would wear out before he was twenty, a palsied
wreck, and die young, while people like Dave ate, drank,
fornicated, played baseball, shook strangers' hands at par-
ties, introducing themselves easily and with a perfectly
steady pulse, and made it without blinking—having had
all kinds of fun—into their eighties or nineties. Sherman
must have inherited his cursed metabolism from his mother.
Worrying and working, she was twice as hyper, ten times
as hyper, as a normal person. He hardly ever saw her
smile, and when she did smile nowadays, it didn't look at
all like a smile, with those scowl lines on her face. But
before the scowl lines, Sherman remembered, when she
was younger and the skin of her forehead was smooth, her
smile had been beautiful and gave off light, like an angel
or a gold-framed Madonna in an art museum.

14

Arnie, it turned out, was able to supply the missing
Chronotron blueprint details, though for a few of them he

had to consult Dr. Klingsturm himself, taking a plane to the great physicist's retreat in Lausanne, because one of the great physicist's eccentricities was that he had a phobia about telephones. "I kip tinkink," confided Dr. Klingsturm in his lovable Katzenjammer accent, "zot a hond vil himerge frim de mout-pizz, tek me by de troat, und drek me bek viddit hinto de vire, ver I vil be treppt fir eterniddy amonk de zignalz und de pipple tawkink aldetime aboud nuttink zigniffikent."

It turned out also, by a great stroke of luck, that Carl Hofstadter still existed and still was president of the university. When the situation was explained to him, he threw up his hands the way he always did and said to Sherm, "It's crazy, you're crazy, we're all crazy, but I'll see what I can do."

"Good old Carl," thought Sherm.

They set up shop in the men's room that had been, in the previous, untampered time line, the control room for the scanoscope. "Well, it's not the best of all possible worlds," sighed Sherm, wrinkling his nose at the smell from the urinals, "but we'll have to make do." The Chronotron itself would be housed in the alley that the men's room window looked out onto; but first—for security —the alley had to be walled up at either end. All this walling—like all the building and assembling of equipment— had to be done secretly, unofficially, because the funds that Hofstadter made available to them came out of places they had no business coming out of, such as faculty pension plans and student government treasuries.

"Carl has the morals of a cat," Sherm said to Arnie as they lay brick, spreading the mortar with trowels, even though they were both full professors, "but his heart's in the right place."

The metaphorical reference to cats occurred to Sherm,

perhaps, because the alley behind Building C was much frequented by that animal. It seemed to be the neighborhood cats' favorite place to mate. The yowling and screeching sometimes became so shrill, the professors had to raise their voices to make themselves heard. But whenever they shooed them out, using brooms, the cats would jump back into the alley an hour or two later, over the uncompleted walls.

"What happens," asked Arnie, rubbing a cat-scratch on his nose, "when we close this place in?"

"The larger parts for the Chronotron," answered Sherm, troweling, "we'll lower from the roof, using pulleys, at night. The rest of it, after we close off the top of the alley, ought to fit through the window of the men's room—excuse me, of the control room."

"No, I mean, what happens to the cats?"

"The cats?" Because Sherm, thinking about the project at hand, and about the unprecedented and mysterious menace hanging over the warp and the woof of all things, had put the nuisance of the cats completely out of his mind.

"The ones that jump back in just before we're done—they'll be walled in," said Arnie.

"True. I didn't think of that. We'll have to shield the terminals and ports of the Chronotron, so the cats don't crawl in there and short anything. Two-inch thick fiberglass ought to do the trick."

"But the cats—the cats will starve to death."

"Yes, I suppose they will."

"That's cruel!"

Sherm put down his trowel and looked the emotional Scot in the eye. "Between you and me, old friend," he said, "I don't like cats. I never did, in this or any other time line. I don't like the way kitty litter smells. Dogs are another story, large dogs, especially collies. If these stupid cats can't take a hint, let them starve to death."

Arnie MacTavish paled. Although an experimental physicist, he was superstitious—perhaps because he had been born and raised in the mist-veiled vales around Loch Shin and there had heard many a thing, and seen one or two, that could not be accounted for in any book of science. . . . Under his breath he muttered: "Wonderful, that's all we need, a Chronotron haunted by the indignant spirits of alley cats. No good, no good will come of it." And the alley, as he laid brick higher and higher, row upon row, began to assume in his eyes the aspect of a long, dark, evil crypt.

15

When the subject of money came up, Sherman's mother always raised her voice, and it was the most piercing voice in the world when it was raised, it went through your head like a spike—in one temple, out the other. His mother's voice would have made a wonderful weapon in a battle, because nothing could withstand it, nothing could block it out, not even a whole pound of cotton plugged in the ears. That voice would leave the enemy helpless on the ground, writhing, begging for relief or the coup de grace. When the subject of money came up, Mom also overdramatized: having to work her fingers raw and bleeding to the bone so that they, her two thoughtless children, but particularly her thoughtless son, could throw money away on comic books, ice-cream sandwiches, and movies. This was an exaggeration. Sherman's comic book collection was sizable, yes, but no more sizable than Ralph's down the street, and it was not even half of what Jason had. Anyway, Sherman hadn't bought a comic book in a year, in more than a year, not since he stumbled onto McGulveyland. And besides, those comic books would be collector's items someday and help pay for college. As for the ice-cream sandwiches, he had been cutting down on them, because of his complexion. With the movies, too, it was no longer the Golden Age, on account of homework, especially lately from Mr. Stammler, who was getting on their case. Last Thursday he had told them they were bad Americans because they didn't know about Francis Scott Key. But Mr. Stammler's angriest voice was soft and dulcet compared to Mom's. Mom's bored through you worse than fingernails scraped across a blackboard or a shriek of feedback on a microphone; then it echoed inside you for hours, sometimes even days, making you shudder and wish you could climb out of your skin. "You think money grows on *trees?*" she would scream. (In McGulveyland occasionally it did.) "You think I *like* working? I work to put *food* on the table, to put *clothes* on your backs. In this world a person has to *work*, and just be thankful, Sherman, Priscilla, that you're *Americans*, that there is work here for you to do, work here for anyone who is willing, because in some parts of the world there *isn't*, in some parts of the world people lie around covered with flies and starve to death by the *millions*, they and their children, by the *millions*, while you blow your allowance on *ice-cream sandwiches*, not even budgeting so you'll have lunch money and bus fare for Thursday and Friday." Which had happened to Sherman only once, and that had been more than a year ago. "Thursday and Friday" was ringing in his head when Dave finally came down the steps with Mary, who wore a long, rustling dress. Her hair looked like a helmet with a flattened spiral on each side. Dave opened the door for her and told Sherman to sit in the back. It was 7:44 now, which meant they wouldn't be getting to Susan's until 7:55 at the soonest. Almost an hour late. Sherman found himself wondering what Fat Clara put away, per week, in ice-cream sandwiches.

16

There was no need, thank God, for conversation, no need to strain in bug-eyed, breathless combat with the stutter demon, because in the car Mary and Susan chattered away and giggled the whole time, not leaving any awful silences. But when they all got out of the car and walked toward the gym, Dave and Mary held hands, and Susan looked at Sherman, so Sherman had to take her hand, which was cold and clammy, and he had to keep holding it until they got to the gym, where they presented their tickets. Taking out his wallet for his ticket gave him an excuse to drop her hand, and he was able to go for a while after that, five or ten minutes, without holding hands, while they walked around and in and out of groups of couples, following Dave and Mary. But then the music started, the D.J. said something, and it was time to hold hands again, for the dancing. Susan's hand reminded him of the slugs on the wall in the back of the house sometimes at night, but of course he couldn't let go of it and wipe his hand on his pants. "I can't really dance," he said to her, turning red and sweating after he stepped on her foot. Susan said confidentially, making a face, "I can't, either. But all you have to do is shuffle around and nobody will notice." And she got closer to him, since it was a slow dance, until her bosom nudged his chest as if they were embracing in public. His problem then was not her hand or stepping on her feet, but pleading with the erection demon not to start up. If the erection demon started up here—it was capable of starting up anywhere—Sherman, surrounded as he was by the entire tenth grade, might as well commit suicide. Jumping off a cliff would be a relief. "You're doing fine," Susan said, and even though she wasn't particularly pretty, he immediately liked her better, despite her hands, almost as if he and she were not on a date but pals in adversity. But he tried to keep her bosom from nudging him, because whenever it nudged him, he felt a door opening inside, and that door, at all costs, had to be kept shut. Behind it pressed this hairy thing with glittering eyes and huge grasping purple-black gorilla hands.

17

When I alighted, my cape fluttering behind me, I found myself on a vast plain on which were mounds, here and there, of what appeared to be mucilage. "So this is dimension X," I thought. Cautiously I probed, bracing myself for a blast of staggeringly ferocious, mind-bogglingly alien psi, but nothing of the sort happened. A few of the mounds of mucilage moved a little, shifted slowly, and I saw now that each of them had a pair of slender knobbed tentacles, like the horns of a snail. I noticed furthermore that the mounds exuded a smell not unlike that of dead leaves and dead fish. These must be, I told myself, the inhabitants of the psi-fiend's home world. The psi-fiend's brothers and sisters, in a manner of speaking. But they were so peaceful, so passive.

With even greater caution I attempted to enter into telepathic communication with them—or with the nearest one, which was about twenty meters away. Impossible.

The creature, if it was indeed thinking, was not thinking in any way I could identify as thought. There was not even the subpsychic hum one receives, back on Earth, from the trees and the grass and even the humble plankton on the bosom of the sea.

Only one thing remained for me to do, and old Borgenicht, I was sure, would have fainted dead away at the suggestion, for this was not only sticking one's head into the lion's mouth, this was climbing inside—completely—and taking up quarters in the lion's stomach. I would become one of these mucilaginous beings. For how else was I to learn what made the psi-fiend tick?

The danger, of course, lay in the difficulty of return. Not only was one buried in the flesh, as it were, of another life-form, but one's very mind—personality and will—became that of the creature. This was not mimicry, this was full noumenal and psychoconsubstantial similitude, and no little cunning was needed to guarantee that one would find the way back, from creature to man—particularly if the creature was reluctant to part with its quintessential itness.

Like a diver over unknown waters I held my nose, muttered a Tantric mantra, set my five-cent turtle to 8:15 P.M. and pulled out the alarm button, its rear right leg, then plunged headfirst into

18

The static on the scanoscope screen cleared after a lot of fiddling with a screwdriver and occasional cursing behind the console from Arnie MacTavish, who had grease smudges on his forehead and whose angry red hair went in all directions—except up, since he was bald on top.

"Good," said Sherm. "Hold it there." And he turned the large directional dial to get a fix on the declination of the flux, then used the optometer controls—on the lower left—to calibrate the chronostat. He checked the calibration by reviewing the Seven Great Moments, an established routine.

The Discovery of the Wheel seemed normal: the caveman Gfarf chopping at the fallen birch limb with his stone ax, looking at the pieces roll down the slanting rock, and grunting to himself thoughtfully.

Everything was as it should have been, also, with Moses on Mount Sinai and with the Crucifixion, though there were a few more clouds in the sky over Golgotha this time. The Fall of Rome was okay—Nero sawing away unmusically on his violin as the smoke billowed up behind him, etc.—and Columbus Setting Foot—

Sherm turned back to the Fall of Rome and zoomed in on a marble stairway to the side. "What do you make of this, Arnie?" he said calmly.

The physicist came around and looked at the screen, then bent forward and looked harder. Cat prints, but much too large for a cat.

"Try another Great Moment," Arnie rasped, clutching the railing near Sherm's chair.

At the Signing of the Declaration of Independence there was an unprecedented giggle in the back of the hall, then someone ran past the signers, almost knocking over Benjamin Harrison, and George Taylor's powdered wig fell off as his mouth fell open.

"A flasher," murmured Sherm, hardly able to believe his eyes. "A flasher."

It was a naked woman with red cat whiskers, and her body was so fabulous that both scientists, full professors though they were and men of the world, spontaneously ejaculated where they stood, in their pants.

Chapter Four

• 1 •

While we still had the strength, I ordered another expedition to the emerald mine—and not because at our last meeting Morgan had suggested the possibility of a native curse. I didn't believe in native curses, ghosts, jinxes, albatrosses, or any kind of extraterrestrial voodoo. A curse might explain the famine on New Batavia but could hardly explain the exact same famine on all the other populated worlds in the known universe, most of which were millions, billions of light-years distant. Mumbo jumbo, like viruses and local customs, didn't cross the hard vacuum. No, I ordered the expedition for the simple reason that any course of action was better than lying on our backs and watching the clouds as we waited for the end.

At the head of the expedition I put Pliscou, since hunger seemed to be gnawing at him more than at the others, like an irritation that eventually drives a man wild. The thorn in the lion's paw, the burr in the horse's saddle. I had visions of Pliscou suddenly frothing at the mouth and becoming red-eyed violent. This new responsibility—to be in charge of our grasping at the final straw of hope—would take his mind off his stomach, I reasoned, and if he did go mad, then at least let him go mad far from the settlement, where he would do less damage and cause less demoralization.

I made Poindexter second in command of the expedition, which comprised a dozen men in all (the number that would fit in our only plane, formerly a lifeboat vehicle on the ship). Poindexter's appointment, too, was by design, because Pliscou hated the exobiologist, and the exobiologist returned the favor—there had been some rivalry between them, over a woman. Let their enmity provide additional distraction.

My place was with the colonists, serving as father figure. I walked around, being visible, looking official, nodding as if to say, "Yes, I know there's a problem, folks, but don't worry, everything's under control." To make it seem like we were doing something, Buster reported to me twice a day on our communication with the expedition (by radio) and with the Guild (by subcom), and then I would tell whoever asked the latest from Pliscou and what Rallston had just said. But I never really told the truth, and no one really wanted to hear the truth, because they already knew it. At the emerald mine there were the same streaked slate fields and rock formations. No new species of fauna, or at least nothing significant—that is, nothing large, intelligent, and malevolent. No sign of a past civilization, no potsherd or piece of missile crusted with verdigris. But our men there kept on digging and sifting, taking readings, using their instruments, and arguing among themselves, and that was fine. As for Rallston, he passed on the news from J846C and Elystria and Beta Centauri, which was no news at all, just the same litany of doom: riots, wars, and revolutions, because people refused to accept the fact that the famine was real and had nothing to do with this government or that economic policy or this social class or that neighboring nation. Nothing to do, in short, with anything human.

Tears welled up in my eyes at the thought that soon we would be leaving—would never see again—not one home but two. First, Earth, poor old Earth, crowded and polluted and weary from all the abuse she had taken over the centuries, yet still with her charm, her slow sunsets at sea or on the desert, the bird song, the smell of pine forests, lilacs in the evening, the hum of mosquitoes—and then this new world under bright Lambda Eridani, filled with enormous, undiscourageable, fast-growing trees, and the small furry dinkers with their silly trumpet noses and awkward scrambling, and the bubbling wide Pickle with its banks riddled with mudworm holes, and the peaceful rhythm, day in, day out, of the crickets and the tree frogs . . .

I ran my fingers through Billy LoBianco's sandy hair, and two weeks later—or was it three?—he was in bed, looking much too thin in the chest and much too big in the belly, his eyes shining as if with fever. His mother had tried to feed him berries, but the berries now vanished the instant they were picked, sometimes even before they were picked. They vanished as one put out one's hand to pick them. Billy, anyway, seemed too weak to eat. He just looked at me with his little freckled face, and I knew what his eyes said: he was waiting for Commander Sherm to save him, as Commander Sherm had saved them all so many times in the past. And everyone now was giving me that same look, following me with their large, feverish eyes, wondering when I was going to save them, so we could get on to the next chapter and a new, more cheerful adventure.

2

Sir Phil's asthma got so bad that finally he had to go home. At the bus terminal we shook hands with him. He looked awful in his civvies: twice as fat, pasty-skinned, down-in-the-mouth, and his hand was limp when I shook it, a pathetic dead-fish hand. Sir Frank turned on his heel and walked away, as if having discharged an unpleasant duty, and Sir Mike, after making a couple of lame jokes, shrugged with embarrassment and, hesitating, followed Sir Frank. But I decided to wait with Sir Phil—Phil, now; he was no longer Sir—until the bus pulled up and he got on. He would need help with his luggage: two enormous trunks, two suitcases, and a tennis racket. It wasn't right for me to abandon the former knight so abruptly, not after all that we had been through together, and in this, his moment of shame. Didn't we all have our moments ot shame, even the best of us?

Noticing my glance at his luggage, which was arranged in a row on the platform, he said with a sigh, "I know, it's silly, so much, but my mother insisted. I didn't need half the stuff."

I nodded, commiserating.

He tried to laugh. "She says, 'What if it rains? What if it snows?' So galoshes, boots. I say, 'Mom, I'm not going to play tennis, I'm going to slay dragons.' But it's like talking to a wall. 'In between dragons,' she says, 'you might have time on your hands. The exercise will do you good, and you'll meet people.' "

I tried to laugh, too.

"You know something, Sherm?" Phil went on, turning to me with a grimace that made his puffy lower lip even puffier. "I can't play tennis worth a damn. I can't move on the court. I'm too fat." He paused to catch his breath. "And there are skis in there, too. Skis—would you believe it?"

To change the subject, I said: "Remember that time when you—in the swimming pool—? Wasn't it funny?"

But he was too busy coughing and spitting phlegm into his handkerchief to hear me.

The bus terminal was a sour-smelling place, dingy and depressing even by Cuspidor standards, and the people in it, waiting like us, all seemed bored to tears, or beyond tears, as if there was no hope of a good time ever again.

"So what will you do now?" I asked, to make conversation.

He shook his head. "I don't know. Mow lawns, maybe —I'm not allergic to grass. I can do that until school starts."

Damned if I was going to ask him about school. Mothers was enough.

I looked at my watch: the bus was twenty minutes late. "You can go," said Phil. "I'll be all right."

But I stuck it out until the gray-and-black coach with the sign AKRON came lumbering around the corner.

I helped him on, helped with the trunks, which must have weighed a ton each, and shook his hand again, trying not to notice how ridiculous he looked. Sir Phil may not have killed a single dragon, but he had been in there trying. You had to give him that. I would miss the kid.

3

Professor Sherm yawned, stretched—and groaned, because his back hurt. And little wonder: he was a bit old to be sleeping on bare stone. Bare stone? He opened his eyes. It was a bright day for a change, and about time, after all that rain. The sun streamed in like gold across the floor of his cave. His cave? He sat up and shook his head to clear it, absently picking a flea out of his armpit and another out of his beard. Christ, he itched. When was the last time he had had a bath?

But wait—there was no such thing as baths, bathtubs, soap, or after-shave.

"Something," he said aloud, in a voice whose harshness surprised him, "is wrong."

Particularly since language hadn't even been invented yet, and here he was talking.

What had happened? It was hard to think before breakfast—for breakfast, today, a brained toad, ugh, and the remains of yesterday's rabbit, all raw, since unfortunately fire wasn't something that happened at one's convenience. He made an effort, though it gave him a headache, to concentrate. Last night, bad dreams: cats, orgasms, chronotrons.

What in the hell was a chronotron? What, for that matter, was a professor? And if Professor Sherm's subject was history, as he dimly remembered it was, then he was out of luck here, because in this time line there was no history, never had been and probably never would be, just a lot of grunting, scratching, and club-carrying, with one day looking pretty much like the next, not counting the variations of sun and rain.

There weren't even cats, since cats were domesticated animals, and domestication, as anybody knew, hadn't been invented either.

With a hoarse howl ex-Professor Sherm got up, grabbed his club, straightened his tattered leopardskin loincloth, and went off—without breakfast—in search of Gfarf.

4

V. Snerk's medicine, to my great surprise, is bitter. Until now his potions have always been sweet or aromatic, or both, like lozenges for a sore throat. But perhaps the potions are the same and *I* have changed. Brrr, what an awful taste in my mouth. I wish he would offer me some of his ice cream to wash it down with (his lime ice cream is the best in the world, in any world; it has essence of cherry blossoms in it). But V. is too busy muttering under his breath about the planet Jupiter and tapping my knee with his little rubber hammer and pulling down my lower left eyelid with his thumb.

"Puberty," he says, which I've heard before.

"It's a fever," I tell him. "Take my temperature."

I must have caught whatever bug this is from one of my adventures, or else from the sex book concealed behind the walnut credenza. Because *Lust Kittens* was undoubtedly breathed over by all sorts of unhygienic individuals before I put my own dirty hands on it and held it near my face, reading. How long can bacteria live on the pages of a paperback? Not long, I think. But perhaps long enough, in McGulveyland. So this fever may actually be—a fit punishment—some kind of book-transmitted venereal disease.

V. places a cool palm on my brow, and I look into his face. Do I detect a flicker of suspicion in those raisin eyes of his? It is hard to read close-set raisin eyes.

"Have you done," he says slowly, reluctantly, "anything you shouldn't have?"

"Yes," I reply in a small voice, feeling extremely young: eight years old, seven, six.

He nods, as if he expected as much, and stirs another

glassful of the medicine. Imagine licorice, cod-liver oil, and pink chalk dust mixed with warm milk and a dash of duck fat. I watch the stuff swirl sickeningly around the bent tin teaspoon, which goes clink-clink-clink against the glass.

"Another one?" I ask, my stomach knotting up. "Do I have to?"

He nods. I sigh, and realize that there will be another glassful after that, and another after that, and so on, glassful after glassful, because the expiation has to equal the sin, and what I did in Mr. McGulvey's library amounts—no question—to a lot of glassfuls.

5

Gfarf sat on a clump of moss with a stupid smile on his face. His stone ax lay at his side, half-buried in daisies and bachelor's buttons. Cylindrical pieces from a birch limb lay, also among flowers, at the base of a large slanting rock nearby. But Gfarf was not plunged in thought, did not muse over the pieces of wood or the inclined plane. He had definitely been distracted at the crucial historical moment, and ex-Professor Sherm, concealed behind a tree, could guess who—what—had distracted him. On one of the caveman's hairy legs was a blob of semen.

Ex-Professor Sherm cursed under his breath. What now? Desperate, he stepped from behind the tree.

"Me friend," he said, pointing at himself. "Friend."

Gfarf blinked and made an animal noise in the back of his throat.

Sherm hitched up his tattered leopardskin loincloth and tried to assume a cheerful, casual air. "Whatcha been doing?" he asked, sauntering over to the rock, though the saunter was not convincing. Back in the Eolithic, or whenever this was, before sidewalks, sauntering probably wasn't known. "Ah," Sherm said. "What's this? Interesting." He picked up a piece of wood. "Very interesting. Notice—round. Round." He held it up for Gfarf to see.

The caveman, following him with his eyes, growled, and his upper lip lifted slightly, showing yellow teeth.

Ex-Professor Sherm, with a nervous laugh, persevered. He put the small birch cylinder on the rock, let it roll down, picked it up again, let it roll again. "See? It's round, it rolls. Isn't that something?"

Gfarf grabbed his stone ax and jumped up, snarling.

"Edgy, aren't you?" Sherm asked, but unfortunately in a voice that was an octave too high to convey calm. "Been fighting too many saber-toothed tigers, I bet. Or do the saber-tooths predate you? No matter. Life, in any case, must be hard. Hand-to-mouth, tooth and claw. I understand. But you see, that's because civilization hasn't been invented yet. They're waiting for you to discover the wheel. The wheel." And he started rolling the piece of wood again on the slanted rock. But Gfarf, evidently reaching the decision that his strange visitor was unwelcome, now advanced menacingly, ax held high.

Sherm backed away. He knew kung fu and tae kwon do—whatever those odd words meant—but had not had his breakfast that day and was feeling weak. It was confusing, too, finding himself like this suddenly in a different time line, whatever a time line was, and his reflexes were probably not up to snuff. With all the crises lately, he hadn't been getting enough exercise. It seemed ages since he had last played tennis with Arnie MacTavish. Whatever tennis was.

"Listen," he said, because he couldn't give up, not with

the warp and the woof at stake, "you probably don't understand what I'm saying, but without the wheel—"

The caveman lunged, roaring, and the roar belched an overwhelming stench of halitosis. Tooth decay in spades. And there wouldn't be dentists or mouthwash for at least ten thousand years. Sherm was almost too nauseated to dodge the ax that came in a rapid arc toward his head.

"If it's round, it rolls, if it's round, it rolls!" he called, fleeing, gesturing, tripping over moss, stones, vines. "And you have to have," he shouted, dodging another blow of the ax, "an axle! Axle! Axle, as in ax!"

Gfarf roared again, enraged at missing, but then they both had to drop everything and run, because a beast emerged from behind a bunch of quince bushes with a roar that far outdid Gfarf's in volume and stink.

"Damn! Another distraction!" thought ex-Professor Sherm, shinnying painfully up an evergreen with sharp, sticky bark, wishing with all his heart that he were back in Building C, whatever Building C was.

6

Without warning, dragons descended on us, catching us in the open, in the parking lot behind the movie theater. Sir Frank dodged a fireball, which bounced and hit my Nelly, and a second later there was a whoosh and she was all on fire, like in a war film. And just when I had got the hang of the stick shift and could pull away without lurching when the light changed.

Sir Mike rolled under another car, taking cover, but it, too, went up in flames, from another fireball, and I prayed that he had been quick enough to get out from under in time, on the other side. What was this stuff they were using on us, napalm?

A dragon swooped low, but I leaped up—a big Baryshnikov leap—with my sword extended, and managed to stab the creature before it could drop a fireball on me. Falling, it careened into a third car, a BMW, which also went whoosh, and I couldn't help laughing a little to myself, imagining the face of the rich guy who would be going to his car when the movie was over, taking out his keys, and finding a gutted black frame in place of his forty thousand dollars.

We ran for an alley filled with garbage cans—Sir Mike, too; he was in one piece; good for him—but from the other end of the alley came men in uniform, shooting. They were dragons disguised as policemen. Which not only tickled their perverted sense of humor but was diabolically clever, because if the real police were drawn by the disturbance, they would conclude, in the heat of the moment, that *we* were the enemy, and would start blasting away not at the dragons but at us.

Not to mention the unfairness of having to fight bullets with swords. The bullets, ricocheting, went zing! zing! around us. It was beginning to look like this would be our final battle, but I said to myself, "All right, then I'll go down swinging," and grabbed a garbage can lid, as if that could serve as a shield, and at the same time started kicking some of the garbage cans, to send them rolling at the enemy. A bullet nicked me in the right elbow; a fireball, from behind, scorched the back of my head, which besides hurting made an awful smell. So I dove right into the fray, figuring that I had only a few seconds anyway and might as well go out in style.

Sir Mike, at my side, joined me in the charge, yelling something like "Geronimo!" which raised my spirits considerably. With our swords we hacked away at the dragon-policemen, who apparently had not expected such élan, because they kept missing us, and some of them stumbled on the rolling garbage cans and fell, which made them look laughable, particularly when their long green tails flopped out of their phony blue suits.

I started to laugh, but just at that moment Sir Mike caught a bullet in his chest, and then another—I saw the holes, two red holes, sudden and circular, exactly as in the movies—and he went down, mouth open. I was prepared for the same, but now on my other side Sir Frank started wielding his sword like a threshing machine on fast forward, and incredibly he felled about five dragons in less than two seconds. There was dragonblood everywhere, smoking. "Wow!" I thought. "He finally got into the act!" But when I looked again, it wasn't Sir Frank at all, it was Sir Josh, as calm as a cucumber and not even breathing hard. There was a professional for you.

A police helicopter—the real police, this time—droned overhead, which made the flying dragons with the napalm quickly leave the scene, and the next thing I knew, we were alone, with steam rising on all sides and bodies all around, and Sir Mike coughing on the ground, twisting a little in pain, as if he had a large splinter that he couldn't get out. Sir Frank and Sir Josh made him comfortable, doing various first-aid things, while we waited for the ambulance to arrive.

"You're wounded, too," Sir Frank said to me.

I looked down at the blood on my arm, and my first thought was, "Maybe I'll get a medal. Won't Mr. McGulvey be proud." But it was probably only what they called "a scratch," because I had no trouble moving my elbow. It tingled a little, that was all. The burn on the back of my head, however, hurt like hell, particularly after Sir Frank brought my attention to it, going "Tsk, tsk." I would

probably have to shave my whole head and apply oint-
ments. I thought of what Terhune had looked like with the
mange.

Sir Frank went with Sir Mike in the ambulance, since
Sir Mike was in no condition to answer questions. All he
could do now was groan feebly, so someone was needed at
the hospital to give the lady at the cashier's window the
wounded knight's social security number, Blue Cross/Blue
Shield card, and date of birth. As they drove off to the
sound of the siren, I shook Sir Josh's hand and thanked
him for his help. "I don't know what we would have done
without you," I said.

Then a chill went slowly up my spine.

"Wait a minute," I said. "Wait a minute. You're dead,
aren't you?"

"Dead?" was his reply, in a voice that I thought, now,
was much too neutral. It wasn't a zombie voice, exactly,
but my remark hadn't even made the man blink.

"It was . . . at the billboard battle, the first battle,
remember?"

He shrugged, as if I had brought up a technicality.

"Hold on," I said, and phased quickly to Mr. McGulvey's
library, quickly checked, and phased back. "Yes, it's on
page 11. Sir Gardyloo told me about it, and then I looked
up at the billboard, and there you were—what was left of
you—in the 'I' of the ZIP, giving off purple wisps . . ."

I half-expected him to say that that wasn't him, that he
had got out of that spot somehow when everyone was
looking the other way, but instead he nodded and said
simply, "You're right. Sorry."

"But wait, where are you going now?"

Sir Josh made a puzzled frown, as if I had asked a
self-evident question. "Well, I don't belong here. You just
said—"

"But you're here . . . I mean, if you leave the adventure . . . Are you going home?" Why was I so concerned? I had hardly known Sir Josh.

He gave a thin smile. "I'm not from outside, like you. There's no home for me when it's over. I just stop." He smiled again, seeing the look on my face. "It doesn't hurt, Sherm. I'm not real, you know, in the first place; I'm just a character in a book."

Was his "stopping," I wondered, like walking off the set of a stage into the unlit wings? It certainly didn't seem to worry him. I was going to tell him that he might as well stick around since he was already here. We could sure use another sword, especially now, with Sir Mike wounded and maybe at death's door. I was going to tell him, damn it, to forget about page 11—who cared anyway, except for a few bent-over copy editors and proofreaders with thick glasses and buckteeth? But the back of my head suddenly ached so badly, I felt it with my hand . . . and Sir Josh was gone.

I looked at my hand: black, completely black, as if I had been cleaning a hibachi with a month's buildup of broiled hamburgers.

7

The smell of dead leaves and dead fish became a different smell: of blankets in a bedroom whose window had not been opened in a hundred years.

I was comfortable for the first time in my life.

I was, only now, safe.

Of course, being no fool, I knew that Sergeant Sherm planned to pull me back as soon as he found out whatever it was he was trying to find out. Smiling, I set up a

Sergeant Sherm lock, which was easy as one-two-three, since I knew him so well—he was myself, after all—and I dusted my hands off, figuratively speaking. So much for Sergeant Sherm.

I took his five-cent turtle, turned it into a little blob of butterscotch tapioca, and flushed it down a black hole on the other side of the J846C galaxy, the granddaddy of black holes. Such a ridiculous toy.

They liked toys, on that disgusting we-world, because they were so weak and helpless.

Holding on to each other—ugh—to keep from falling down. Breathing each other's we-breath all the time, talking, making contacts, contracts. It gave me the willies.

I felt sorry for George, who was stuck there. Though it was his own fault, poking his nose, figuratively speaking, into that fault.

It didn't pay to get overconfident. Just because there hadn't been a real fault Here in three centuries. The faults, Here, were the only threat. The only weather. The only indeterminate variable.

Poking one's figurative nose into things was not normal. George had probably been sick, having his period. And it was just rotten bad luck that the fault had to happen then, and that it had been a real fault this time, and that it had happened only a stone's throw away . . .

But overconfident or sick, or both, it was no figurative skin off my figurative nose. Too bad for George. George was George, I was I. And I was Here.

I slid along in peace. You wouldn't catch me sneaking peeks into places I didn't belong. No, sir. Not a chance, period or no period. I liked it Here. With any luck, I would last eight, nine, ten millennia, and then—translation. I had it made.

8

Once, when Terhune got distemper and a lot of his hair
fell out in clumps and all he would do all day was lie
on his side panting, Mom said that they would give the
medicine one more week, and then, if it still didn't work,
the dog would have to be put to sleep, because she had
already spent three hundred dollars on the vet and no
animal was worth three hundred dollars, unless maybe
you were a breeder and had pedigree papers. Sherman
was sure that Terhune would be put to sleep, since according to everybody distemper was fatal. Mrs. Pieczynski's
collie had died from it last summer, and the Burbanks'
funny half-retriever half-German shepherd, Sammy, who
used to go exploring in the woods with them behind the
movie theater, his tail always wagging, had died from it
the year before that. So Sherman spent a lot of time up in
his room with his comic books, to take his mind off the
death of his best friend. He reread all the old Supermans,
Batmans, Popeyes, and Little Lulus, going downstairs only
for lunch and supper. And it worked: he forgot all about
the dog. But he forgot all about his errands, too, and got
hell from Mom. She threatened to take the comic books
away from him, burn them, if he didn't shape up. She was
capable of doing it, too; she was capable of almost anything when she lost her temper. Sherman could see the
headline: MOM, IN RAGE, MURDERS SON. In smaller type:
PENN HILLS TEENAGER BUTCHERED WITH CARVING KNIFE. 23
PIECES. The story: "He didn't get the milk and bread,"
said Mrs. Maureen Potts of 23 Westbrook Avenue. Mr.
Clifford Potts, Mrs. Potts's husband, was unavailable for
comment, having departed from the home five years before without warning and leaving no forwarding address.

Not so much as a postcard. The judge found this a highly
mitigating circumstance. "Think of the burden she was
under," he instructed the jury, "having to raise two unpleasant children by herself, with no help from anyone.
The Wisconsin relatives all turned up their noses. Only
Uncle Benny, from Coral Gables, sent a check on birth-
days, and that wasn't for much. Twenty dollars nowadays,
what can you buy with it? A pair of jeans? A shirt? Barely."
The distraught Mrs. Potts, tears now rolling down her
wrinkle-covered cheeks, went on: "He kept having to be
reminded to take out the garbage. Repeatedly, he went to
school without making his bed. He hit his sister." The
ladies and gentlemen of the jury shook their heads, went,
"Tsk, tsk." Mom's voice rose in a courtroom crescendo:
"He didn't do anything, he sat around all day reading
those goddam stupid comic books. I just couldn't take it
any longer." "Case dismissed!" said the judge, quivering
with indignation, bringing his walnut gavel down with
tremendous force, perhaps wishing that Sherman could be
sewn together and reanimated so he could cut the little
bastard up into twenty-three pieces himself, or beat him
to a pulp then and there with his gavel, to a pulp the
consistency of butterscotch tapioca, while the jury applauded
and the reporters went "Pop, pop!" with their old-fashioned
flash cameras. Sherman lay in his bed like a stone. What
could he do now, not allowed to read comic books? There
was nothing to do, nothing, without Terhune. He was so
bored, he felt like screaming. Instead, he sighed. He
sighed again. He sighed twenty-three times, each time
with increasingly intense ennui. That was how he discov-
ered phasing. All phasing was was sighing hard enough. I
found myself in a green meadow like something out of
Elvish Olde England, with Heidi's Alps in the distance,
lilac mist at the edges—but went back like a rubber band.

It took Sherman almost a year to get the hang of it, to master the technique, There was nothing in the local library, not one book on the subject.

9

Arnie pulled him on board the ship by the scruff of his neck.

"Phew," said the Scotsman, nose wrinkling. "No offense, Sherm, but you stink to high heaven."

Sherm, in his foul leopardskin loincloth and with black sticky sap and pine needles all over his hands and legs—and having been stranded for what seemed ages in that godforsaken, fleabitten corner of the Eolithic if not earlier—did not take offense. "I was trying to get the wheel invented," he grunted, "but I had no luck. It was horrible. But how, in that case, did you . . ."

"Well, most of the time lines in the present did wink out, and the few remaining ones got unbelievably twisted. By sheer coincidence, as I was within a hair's-breadth of winking out myself, who should pop by, in this neat silver flying saucer-runabout, but an Arnie MacTavish, complete with red goatee, from the twenty-third century. . . ."

"Excuse me, old friend, but do you have anything to eat?" Sherm asked, sitting up and scratching himself. "I went without breakfast today, and fleeing irate cavemen and prehistoric beasts does give a person an appetite."

The physicist smiled, turned, opened the small fridge, and frowned. "Now, that's odd."

"What's odd?"

"I could have sworn . . ." He shrugged. "Here's a wedge of Swiss cheese. That'll have to do."

"Wonderful," murmured Sherm, accepting the plastic-wrapped piece of food with both hands, as if it were manna. "It beats all hell out of raw toad and day-old fly-covered rabbit."

"Hm, yes, but I could have sworn we had a couple of lamb chops here, in tinfoil. I put them there myself. Could have heated them up for you in no time. Curious . . . Oh well, no matter."

Chewing, Sherm asked: "And this Arnie MacTavish from the future, what happened to him?"

Arnie moved away a little, wincing from the body odor given off by his colleague. He ran his fingers through his red goatee. "It's complicated. So complicated, in fact, that I gave up trying to figure it out, and you know how much I like to figure things out. I gave up after the third loop."

"Loop?"

"You know, time loop. There were time loops, loops inside loops, figure eights, paradoxes, a veritable Möbius strip—or perhaps Klein bottle—of probabilities and potentialities all tangled up. Tangled so badly, it would have been too much even for Escher himself."

"And who is Escher?"

"Ah, dear fellow," said Arnie, sadly shaking his bald head. "You've been away from civilization too long. A sorry pass, this, for a historian. Doesn't know who Escher is. But it will come back to you, it will come back to you. After a good hot bath, and you get into some decent clothes . . ."

"And Building C? Is it still . . ." Sherm pressed his temples with his index fingers, trying to think.

"But we were talking, I believe, about my alter ego from the twenty-third century."

"Yes, sorry. Is it important?"

"Important? No, but it's complicated. So complicated, in fact, that—"

"You said that already."

"I did indeed. It's from being in those loops, I'm afraid. One goes around and around. I've become repetitive."

Sherm, still famished, asked for something else to eat.

10

I'm in trouble now. I can't find *Lust Kittens*. I looked everywhere. It's not behind the walnut credenza, not behind any of the other books, not under the cabinets or under the armchairs or under the rug. Yes, that's how worried I got, I even looked under the braided rug. Finally I took a deep breath and held a council of war with my thoughts. Thinking, I remembered that the books in Mr. McGulvey's library change, they change every week. This must mean that *Lust Kittens* has changed, too. The magic library probably considered that the paperback belonged, that it was just another of Mr. McGulvey's books. Though, of course, it doesn't belong, not at all. . . . And now, I ask myself, if it's been changed, what has it been changed into? I can't help feeling that I've introduced a foreign body into the system, and that there will be consequences. . . . This library is so innocent. What will happen with *Lust Kittens* in its bookish bloodstream? There's a cold lump in the pit of my stomach. After Mr. McGulvey's hospitality, his trust in me . . .

I start looking in the other adventures, the ones I know, to see if they've changed, if they've been affected. Although I can't put my finger on it—there's no direct, clear evidence—I get the impression that something's wrong, all right. Contamination has taken place. You can almost smell it.

11

Susan, in the car, expecting to be kissed, because Dave and Mary were kissing like pros in the front seat, lifted her face to Sherman, bent her neck a little, and pointedly stopped talking. Sherman should have kissed her then, because he was feeling comfortable with her, more comfortable than he had felt all evening, having got through the dancing and the clammy hand-holding and even the bosom-nudging without making an excruciating, everlasting fool of himself. But instead of kissing her, he hesitated. Then of course, to disguise this ridiculous hesitation, he pretended that he didn't understand that kissing was required of him now, though it was so obvious that anyone who didn't understand something as elementary as that would have had to be a drooling imbecile. Minutes passed, and the more minutes that passed, the more mortified Sherman became. In a strangled voice he tried to make conversation about . . . what did they have in common? who did they both know? . . . Fat Clara, she was the only one—so Sherman talked, in his worst machine-gun stuttering way, about how much Fat Clara weighed and the fact that she was bigger than her father now, Mr. Davidov. Susan gave him a pained-disgusted look, and Dave turned around and told him to shut up, then went back to kissing Mary, who all this time was as silent as a wall. Mary's hair, Sherman noticed, no longer looked like a helmet; strands and curls stuck out in places, as if she had been in a fight. Later, when it was time to drop her off, she spent forever, more than ten minutes, combing and patting her hair, holding up a pocket mirror as she combed and patted, before she got out and went up the steps with Dave. What did Dave see in her? She was so boring, as boring as a wall.

But, then, Dave didn't really see anything in anybody; for him other people were amusement, mild amusement, nothing more. This was the reason he could be so calm at a dance or in a car kissing. It didn't matter to Dave, just as it didn't matter when he hadn't done his homework, or even the time he was called to the principal's office because of the joke they had played—he, Frank, and Al—on the new kid from France, urinating into the kid's hall locker in the middle of fifth period, after Mrs. Baker had made such a big thing, in front of everyone, of how beautifully the kid pronounced *eau de cologne* and *parfumerie*. "Let's give Frenchie some *parfum!*" they said, chortling. Dave was always smiling slightly, as if he were watching the world on television and could get up at any time and go to the kitchen for a Coke and pretzels. When Sherman unlocked and opened the door, he heard the television on: Priscilla the Pill was sneaking a movie—cops and robots—way past her bedtime, and Mom should be home from her class anytime now. When Sherman went to turn off the set, Priscilla the Pill screamed and threatened; he turned it off anyway and pointed upstairs, his face impassive and squinting like a merciless Clint Eastwood or Charles Bronson about to pump lead into a junkie. Priscilla the Pill, furious, ran and turned the set back on. He turned it off again. She kicked him and ran screaming upstairs as he tried to catch her and slug her. Her door slammed; he started to shoulder it open before she had time to lock it, but then the phone rang and he had to go answer it. It was Susan, inviting him to the movies next weekend. Her dad would drive them. She didn't really like double dates. He agreed with her. Then they got into a conversation about nothing much, but it made him feel so comfortable that he told himself that if the situation ever came up again where he had to kiss her, he would have no problem, even though she wasn't, to tell the truth, that pretty.

12

"They're time witches," Arnie MacTavish told him.
Sherm blinked. "What?"
"Time witches."
"What in creation are time witches?"
"I learned about them from myself from the twenty-third century."
"Arnie, physicists, no matter what century they come from, don't believe in witches."
"They wreak havoc on the male endocrine system. It has something to do with displacement/diffraction of the Fraunhofer lines. I can't see what possible connection there could be, to be honest, between the spectrum of the sun and one's testicles. But in the loop we were in, my future self and I, there wasn't time, you understand, for lengthy explanations. They evolved from cats."
"What cats? They're naked women!"
"On an alternate Earth of low probability. Which, incidentally, is the only way we can get out of this mess."
"What way? You've lost me again. Incidentally, I could use a shave. And a bath. And flea powder, if you have it."
"Ah—of course."
The flying saucer-runabout may have been short on food, but it had every convenience, and before long Professor Sherm felt human and looked human. He wiggled his toes in the hot water and sighed. The itchy beard had come off with a pleasant hum from a twenty-third-century gadget that looked like a yellow toy telephone, and his

face now was clean, smooth, and scented. He hadn't been this comfortable in years. He fell asleep.

And dreamt that he was in a woods hunting time witches. His strategy was to use a wedge of Swiss cheese on a string, pulling it slowly toward him, and when a time witch jumped out from behind a tree to pounce on the cheese, he would let loose with his 12-gauge shotgun. The problem was, if he got too good a look at the time witch—and it was difficult not to grab a hungry eyeful of such fabulous female flesh, albeit of feline origin—he would ejaculate at the same moment he pulled the trigger, and that tended to spoil his aim. On the other hand, it was not easy—it was virtually impossible—to aim without looking. As a result, he wasn't killing many time witches, and how else was the woof and the warp to be saved?

"I'm on the horns of a dilemma," he thought.

"And no wonder," said Arnie MacTavish at his side. "Look at the bait you're using. Cheese. Cheese is for mice, not cats."

Sherm felt extremely stupid in his dream. "My mind's still clouded," he thought, "from being in the Eolithic. I need a vacation. I need to play some tennis and read the morning paper over a cup of coffee."

13

The warted Frops, with the ululating "Caroo!" that was their war cry, poured out from behind the crenels and merlons of the battlements overhead, jubilant that they had so successfully ambushed and surrounded us. Princess Martha Anne, Sir Gardyloo, and I were indeed caught by surprise. We hadn't a weapon, not so much as an ornamental dirk, between us, while each Frop (being seven-armed) brandished seven broadaxes, maces, and/or spears.

"Damn," cursed Sir Gardyloo under his breath, "We signed the treaty with them only last Wednesday. The dirty double-crossers!"

"This," I said with a sangfroid anyone would have envied, "is what I call a tight spot."

The enemy advanced slowly on all sides, coming down the steps, though many took up stations on the battlements, their bows and arrows trained on us. The Frops were savoring the moment. You could tell from the way they batted their eyes, the eyes that went all around their heads, and from the way their pointed tongues hung and dripped.

In the center of the courtyard the three of us stood back-to-back (or, actually, shoulder-to-shoulder-to-shoulder, forming an equilateral triangle), and out of the corner of my eye I saw the Princess assume her fighting crouch, which looked incongruous, almost comical, in her fancy farthingale. I wondered how we were going to get out of this one.

We always did, somehow; we always managed to turn the tables and save our skins at the last minute. That, after all, is the nature of cliff-hangers. But this tight spot really looked hopeless. There was nothing that could be used as a shield. No garbage can lid. And unless the ground opened up beneath us or a giant bird came out of the sky and picked us up—which would make the plot blatantly deus ex machina and therefore boring—there was no exit. No side door, trapdoor, tunnel, well, ladder, alley, balcony to jump off, or rope to swing away on.

Then they stopped advancing, and the head warted Frop came forward. He was the ugliest one of them all. His eyes were puffy and his thick, veined hands were purple-black gorilla hands. "We—let—you—go," he rumbled. "You—give—us—girl."

Girl? I almost laughed. Did he mean Princess Martha Anne? She was no girl. She was a Moh warrior, an Elinak priestess, and a Llasghorian-Finsterfeld adept. Even in a farthingale and without as much as a nail file, she would be able to take out half the Frop army—all by herself—before she fell.

"What do you want with her?" Sir Gardyloo asked, which I thought an awfully inappropriate question.

I jabbed him with an elbow and whispered out of the side of my mouth: "What's the matter with you? We can't abandon the Princess, we're a team." Why, she had saved his life, and mine, at least a dozen times in just the past month.

The Frop made a sound like an evil chuckle. "We—long—time—away—from—wives," he said. "Get—plenty—horny—on—campaign. Need—much—screw."

Princess Martha Anne, in her fighting crouch, hands poised and cupped, didn't blink, didn't even pale. "What incredible discipline," I thought.

I was going to sputter something in indignation and defiance, such as, "How dare you, vile, unclean, warty excrescence!" Because these creatures, and I'm not exaggerating, made even toads look handsome. But Sir Gardyloo said:

"And we'll go free?"

I could hardly believe my ears. What treachery! To save his skin, he was willing to . . . I was glad, in that moment, that I had killed him in the other story, the one with the dragons of Cuspidor, even though that had been an accident. But who would have dreamed, after all we had been through together, that at heart, underneath, when the chips were down, when push came to shove, he was no friend, no true knight, but just another rotten, scurvy, self-serving . . . I spat.

"Don't be so old-fashioned," he whispered to me. "This way we get off with our lives."

"And Princess Martha Anne?"

"So? It's only sex. It won't kill her."

"With a whole army of these revolting warted Frops? And they *smell*!" They smelled the way Terhune did when he used to roll in carrion (before the development went up across the street and all the woods were bulldozed down). The Frops smelled even worse than that.

The Princess said nothing. She was like a statue.

"Look, Sherm," Sir Gardyloo said, his lips touching my ear. "If I get killed in this adventure, I have to practice the piano for my lesson tomorrow. I have to do scales. A half an hour of scales, the teacher says, with a metronome. I *hate* scales. My fingers are too short and fat, they don't move right. When I sit at the keyboard, I feel like screaming. And here, what's happening here, come on, is just in a book. It's not real."

"You'd never be able to live with yourself afterward," I said.

"That's bullshit, Sherm. Come on, be honest. You wouldn't mind that much seeing the Princess get laid by a couple hundred yucky monsters."

That's when I realized that this story was turning kinky. I punched Sir Gardyloo in the nose as hard as I could and charged the head warted Frop, crying, "Over my dead body!" Though a cynical voice said, in my mind, that that was all well and good, but *I* didn't have a half an hour of scales waiting for me back in reality. The last thing I saw, in this spoiled adventure, which could have been a lot of fun if it hadn't gone bad, was a spear sticking *boingg!* in my chest and a row of leering Frops slowly unzipping their flies. The picture winked out, and then all I had for a while was a sharp pain that made it impossible to breathe, as if I had jumped into ice water.

Chapter Five

• 1 •

Mr. McGulvey tells me a story—we're on the porch, having pink lemonade with Camembert on crackers—but the story is poky and roundabout, so I don't pay attention, and it's maybe a half an hour before it dawns on me that what he's really been trying to do is tell me something through the story. But what? What has the story been? I have no idea—my ears shut down some time ago, almost as if I were sitting in Mr. Stammler's class. Poky, roundabout stories do that to me. I can't help it. Mr. McGulvey himself seems to be aware of the problem. But he can't speed up or get to the point or just give me the message straight, without a story. I'd like to unburden him of whatever the message is, but don't know how. It must be important, too, because he's never talked at such length before.

He starts again, tries another tack. Something about the Independence of Africa and Old Corduroy. Now, that's interesting. What does Old Corduroy have to do with Africa? I perk up. But the realization that Mr. McGulvey is finally having a man-to-man talk with me, which may well lead to Honesty, the Facts of Life, and *Lust Kittens*, is so unnerving that instead of listening, all I can think about is girls, pornography, and how hard it is for a healthy teenage boy to be a virgin.

"And this receptionist in the desert, she turned out to be a powerful witch," Mr. McGulvey goes on. "She took off her glasses and cursed Corduroy, told him he would be a schoolboy all his life, a schoolboy no matter how old he got."

With a wince I think: He's alluding to my lack of maturity. Telling me it's time I grew up.

"She was unforgiving, you see."

I think: Maybe he'll forgive me, and everything will go on as before. If that happens, I promise, I swear I'll turn over a new leaf and never again—

"Even though it was just a harmless prank. Corduroy doesn't have a mean bone in his body."

I think: And I, too, was not out to hurt anyone. It's just this all-consuming biology problem. Yes, I ought to be forgiven. Boys will be boys.

With such thoughts continually interfering, I never do find out what connection there is between the curse on Old Corduroy by the receptionist witch in the desert and the Independence of Africa. Something about betrayal, I think, though I doubt Mr. McGulvey came out and used so strong a word. I ask myself: And am I a Judas, with that paperback? But the betrayal doesn't seem to refer to me; it is a betrayal of a subtler kind, where the villain and the victim turn out to be the same person. Something deep, in other words, with a little Freud and a little philosophy in it.

Bubble and Squeak drop by, holding hands.

"What a nice day!" says Bubble. "What a lovely view!"

Bubble has a way of stating the obvious—of course it's a lovely view, with the gorse, the picturesque precipice, the lilac mist. In anyone else's mouth, "What a lovely view!" would sound dim-witted, but Bubble's enthusiasm is so pure, you look at the view again, and it's as if you didn't know how lovely it was, but you do now, because he said it with his eyes sparkling and cheeks flushed.

Mr. McGulvey drops the subject that was between us, glad for the excuse. He takes out a large checkered handkerchief and gently mops his forehead.

2

I visited Sir Mike in the hospital. He was in good spirits, cracked jokes, and showed discomfort only once, when he had to cough. The mayor of Cuspidor came by with a bunch of flowers and a silver medal for Sir Mike, and sat with us a while, though obviously he was a very busy man. At one point he took out a large checkered handkerchief and gently patted his brow. I was bothered by this gratuitous repetition—it wasn't at all hot in the room, and no one was sweating—but I remained in character and said nothing. A nurse asked us to leave, so we all said encouraging things to Sir Mike, shook his hand, and left. Sir Frank and I went back to the station, where we held a glum council of war, there being only two of us now.

"What's the use?" said Sir Frank in an oddly bored, flat voice, as if reciting something he had rehearsed too often. "There's nothing we can do. The dragons have won."

"If we give up," I said, "who will there be to defend the people of this metropolis? The men, the women, the innocent children?"

Sir Frank shrugged.

"We can't give up," I protested, "There must be some way to stop the dragons. If not by the sword, then . . . by other means."

Sir Frank raised an eyebrow. "What other means?"

"I don't know. We have to think. We have to use our imagination. To be creative."

But he shut his eyes and made a sour face, as if to say, "I've heard this before."

I went out and took a walk, to help me think. What Achilles' heel did the dragons have? I passed a small park filled with litter and squirrels, the squirrels jumping from one piece of litter to another in their endless search for food. One squirrel, sitting up, had a pizza crust in its mouth. I thought of Sir Gawain, how he had loved pizza, and how his face had looked in death, glowing like the Moon on his hospital pillow, and suddenly I felt uneasy about Sir Mike being alone there, unprotected. What prevented the dragons from sneaking into the hospital— the token security would present no obstacle to them— and doing away with the wounded knight?

Back at the hospital, running down the corridor to Sir Mike's room, I found myself at the end of the hall, where the elevators were. How could I have missed his room? I backtracked all the way to the nurses' station. Was I on the wrong floor? In the wrong wing? I asked the nurses for directions, and was surprised by their confusion.

"It should be . . . around here," said one of them, gesturing vaguely at a door marked INCINERATOR.

"I want to talk to the commander!" cried a man from another room, coming out, waving his arms. It was Jack Cuthbertson. What in the hell was Jack Cuthbertson doing here? "Ned says he found a cache of baked beans, but the bastard won't tell us where!"

I turned my back, to blot out this distraction. I focused on the door. Wasn't it a little odd that garbage here was disposed of down an incinerator chute, as if this were an apartment building? And didn't the word INCINERATOR look awfully new?

Jack grabbed me by the arm, to get my attention.

I hissed at him out of the corner of my mouth: "You don't belong here. Can't you see that? This is a hospital, not New Batavia."

Jack looked around, saw the nurses, and his indignation about the baked beans Ned was allegedly hoarding disappeared (a ridiculous charge, anyway, because Ned would never have done such a thing, he was as honest as they came; and besides, why should some cache of baked beans be alone exempt from the mysterious and universal plague that had befallen us?). "Uh, sorry, Commander," he said, turning red and stepping back.

I couldn't be angry with him. This seeping contamination of adventures was my fault, not his. If only it didn't get worse. But back to business.

I opened the door, fearing I knew not what, and jumped aside as a ceiling-high wall of trash came tumbling down. This was an incinerator-chute room after all. No, wait, it wasn't—the garbage went on and on, it didn't stop at a wall, and the room was not closet-sized, it was big, a regular hospital room. Sir Mike's room. I dove in, dove through the endless trash, plastic bags, soiled newspaper, milk cartons, empty cans of soap, dog food, precooked spaghetti. It took forever to reach the bed.

"Sir Mike!" I cried. "Are you all right?"

He wasn't breathing. His broad chest, his muscular arms were motionless, like stone. The dragons had buried him in trash, then put the INCINERATOR sign on the door, probably snickering to themselves all the while.

Of all the knights, I had liked Sir Mike the best. And now only Sir Frank and I were left. I swallowed hard, forced myself not to blubber in front of the nurses, and numbly headed back to the fire station. I forced myself to think. There had to be a way to wrest victory from the jaws of defeat. There had to be.

Then, at last, an idea came to me.

3

Mr. Stammler cleared his throat, went, "Ahem," and began talking about Aaron Burr. You would have thought it would be interesting, since it had to do with treason, but it was just like everything else in American history—dates, taxes, congressional acts, resolutions, treaties, and then more dates to put in your notebook. Dates made Sherman's ears shut down. He wished he could become not a doctor, a lawyer, or a banker, but a great traitor. Make everyone's mouth fall open in shock. Stab the President in the back after shaking his hand, trample the flag underfoot, give all our military secrets to the Soviet Union, blow up the Statue of Liberty on the Fourth of July, and know with a smile that in millions of living rooms, bedrooms, and family rooms across the nation, from Maine to California, wherever there was a television set, your name is more despised, more reviled than Hitler, Judas, and Charles Manson rolled into one. Sherman, sick of hearing about democracy and the Bill of Rights, phased to

4

Washington, D.C., where George, the psi-fiend, was murdering one gray-haired legislator after another, and you could hardly blame him for lashing out at the abomination of we-weakism that characterized this strange, revolting world whose inhabitants were too tiny, numerous,

nd jerky in their movement over the ground. Deaf and
lind in the ways that mattered, they relied on gizmos for
everything, even to tell the time and wake up in the
morning.

Where was mystic champion Sergeant Sherm, to defend
he Land of the Free and the Home of the Brave even
hough he came from gloomy Scotland? Alas, buried in the
owels of an alien denizen of dimension X, immobilized
nside a mound of ego-centered mucilage.

Where was his trusty five-cent turtle, to pull him out of
hose bowels and that mucilage at 8:15 sharp in the P.M.,
ts rear right leg ringing? Buried, alas, even more irre-
rievably than its owner, for it lay at the very bottom of
he very deepest black hole in the J846C galaxy, and even
f one had been able to retrieve it thence, the alarm-turtle
vas useless, for it was a turtle no longer, rather a blob,
urtle-shaped, of tapioca, butterscotch, which can make no
ound remotely like ringing, only a wet glurp as the spoon
poons it from the cup, and a wetter glurp as the mouth
akes it, tongues it, half-chews it, and swallows it, gulp,
own a black esophagus to a blacker stomach and eventu-
lly to the blackest of black interiors, the bowels, ante-
hamber to the colon of doom and the final, malodorous,
ucking wet flush to nothingness.

5

The static on the scanoscope screen refused to clear,
hough Professor Sherm banged the side of the console
vith his fist. "Damn!" he said. "We have only three min-
tes, and the thing won't work!" The light in this brief
ubble of probability that contained Building C and the
hronotron (Chronotron Number 3, now, or was it Num-

ber 4?) was already beginning to dim, and the Cherenkov radiation that played about the large chrome accumulators seemed unconvinced, somehow, of its own reality.

"Maybe they use direct current in this time line," said Arnie MacTavish, pulling nervously on his red goatee.

"Can't you do something? You're the scientist."

"Without an adapter . . ." Arnie muttered. The truth was that he, like so many theoretical physicists, was helpless when it came to plugs, outlets, pigtails, grounds, and Wheatstone bridges.

Professor Sherm picked up the phone and hurriedly dialed Carl Hofstadter, but the university president was out—on vacation in the Berkshires, said his assistant. With two minutes to go—"How I hate these down-to-the-wire situations," said Professor Sherm under his breath—he dialed overseas, to Dr. Klingsturm, but there was no such number, and the operator had never heard of Lausanne, or Switzerland, or, for that matter, Europe.

"He has an extremely thick accent," offered Professor Sherm, breaking into a sweat as he watched the second hand on the wall clock advance. "He talks funny."

"A lot of people here," said the operator, "talk funny."

Wherever *here* was.

There were forty-five seconds to go when Professor Sherm hung up. He forced himself to think. If the chronostats could be shunted serially . . . He threw a switch here, a switch there, going more by feel or intuition than sense. And Arnie . . . Arnie wasn't doing anything, just standing and tugging on his red goatee.

"What's the matter with you?" asked Professor Sherm as he threw more and more switches. "Why aren't you helping? You know this machine better than I do." But then he thought a little, with part of his mind, as he tried to calculate the retrotemporal differentials—it was amazing now clearly his mind worked, in this crisis, with only fifteen seconds now to go before the bubble winked out on them—and said: "Unless you're not Arnie MacTavish at all, but that other Arnie MacTavish, from the twenty-third century."

The Scot squirmed, looked away, and finally chuckled. "You found me out. But it's too late now."

Ten seconds.

"But why?" asked Professor Sherm, still working desperately at the controls, his back to his friend—or, rather, to his friend's treacherous future double. "Surely you people in the twenty-third depend upon the integrity of the Continuum as much as we."

Five. Four.

"In our line," explained the false Arnie MacTavish, "the Chronotron isn't reconstituted until *after* the time witches destroy the—"

Two.

The screen cleared, due to a purely fortuitous concatenation of switch-throwings, and they saw the Signing of the Declaration of Independence, but this time there was no Benjamin Harrison or George Taylor in a powdered wig. The signers were all African chieftains in leopardskins and wearing necklaces made of shark teeth and bear claws. The Africans had bones in their noses, too, so Professor Sherm knew immediately that this was not the twentieth century. One of the chieftains in the back row, apart from his skin color, bore an uncanny resemblance to V. Snerk.

6

V. Snerk closes his office, locks all the locks, and takes me to a door in the side of a hill. Entering, we go down a

long staircase to a subway station. I had no idea there was
a subway system in McGulveyland. I think of McGulveyland
as not exactly wilderness but not developed, either; a
realm with little in the way of technology. One expects
magic places to be unspoiled: bucolic, with greensward.
But down here everything is in chrome and Plexiglas. A
train goes through—not our number, so we wait on the
platform—and the cars of the train are modern and noise-
less as they pass. In one of the windows I catch a glimpse,
for less than a second, of a naked woman with cat whiskers. She is naked, at least, from the waist up, that's all I
see of her, two big gorgeous globe-breasts. I have to exert
all my willpower not to ejaculate. Even then, it's a near
thing. Does V. notice my trouble? If he does, he pretends
not to, his needle nose in a train schedule. (Though why
he brought a schedule, I don't know. We're probably
going to visit his sick cousin in Barnett-by-the-Gulf, and
all trains stop there.)

So the worst has happened, unless my guilty imagination is playing tricks on me. The lust kittens—time
witches—have broken out of the book, broken out of the
library, and are now spreading their anarchy everywhere.
Will any place be safe from them? Will things that I love
here—the fuzzy palm trees on the roofs of the villages, the
unusually gawky storks that nest in the fuzzy palm trees,
and the six-or-seven-decker pagodas with church bells that
play Top 40 tunes in minor keys—will they all start winking out? Will V. Snerk wink out?

I tug at his sleeve, to warn him, to alert McGulveyland
to the threat. But he ushers me into a car on the other
side of the platform, and I have to devote all my attention
to the difficulty of walking in public as inconspicuously
as possible despite the fact that I'm almost half bent
over, because the erective effect of seeing the time witch

has not worn off, is showing no signs of wearing off.

We ride to another station, transfer to a different-color train, emerge from a tunnel, go over a bridge, and arrive finally at a town, where a crowd of people in special dress and flowers greet us. This is not Barnett-by-the-Gulf, and we're not visiting anyone sick; rather, we've been invited to a baby-naming. These people, too, are relatives of V. Snerk, but on the other side of his family (whatever side that is). And I'm the guest of honor, it turns out, because I come from so far away. I'll be presiding over the ceremony.

The day passes in a constant blush as I'm introduced to an endless number of cheerful and dignified persons of both sexes and all ages. They're in their Sunday best. In McGulveyland, apparently, a baby-naming is as important as a wedding. Just about everyone I'm introduced to asks with concern if I'm having back trouble, and they suggest remedies: hot pads, poultices, pills. V. himself shows no interest in this, though he's a doctor and an expert on poultices. I blush and blush; the sweat pours off my forehead. My handkerchief is soaked.

The baby, only a few days old, is surrounded by yellow silk in all sorts of decorative folds and bows. It's adorable, making bubbles with its little mouth and clawing the air with its little dimpled hands the way babies do. The people present me with the baby. They want me to hold it. I shake my head no, no, but they insist. I'm supposed to hold the baby through the whole ceremony.

Even in normal circumstances, when I can stand straight, I hate holding babies. They're boring, they smell like cheese and BM, and they're more fragile than eggs. If you don't hold a baby just right, it can suffocate, or a little bone somewhere may snap, or its little skull—which is so thin and soft that you can actually see the pulse inside its head—might get dented, leaving it brain-injured for life, and then the parents sue you for millions of dollars. If the baby suddenly barfs or makes a load in its diaper, you can't flinch and let go of it, either, because there's nothing in the world worse than dropping a baby.

The mayor, in high boots and an official-looking coat with large silver buttons, each button depicting a different military scene, a sea battle, hands me the baby. I scarcely breathe, holding it. Fortunately, the thing doesn't squirm or start bawling; it continues making little bubbles and clawing the air, as if there was nothing abnormal about its being in the arms of a teenager with a gutter mind. After this, I swear to myself, by all that's holy, I'll never touch an X-rated paperback or magazine again.

The mother and father of the baby, neither one looking the least bit like V. Snerk, come up and say their lines. I'm blushing too hard to pay attention, but assume that my part in the ceremony is only to hold the baby, that I don't have to say anything. I'm wrong. The mayor leans over to me with a kindly smile and explains in my ear: I'm supposed to name the baby.

"But . . . what is its name?" I ask, my face like an oven.

"The baby doesn't have a name," the mayor says politely, still smiling. "That is why it needs one." And the parents nod and smile, too.

They are all waiting for me to name this baby. I am dumbfounded. I look for V. Snerk in the crowd. He is off to the side, discussing cusps and zodiacal houses with a gentleman as bald as himself.

Is the baby a boy or a girl? The yellow wrappings tell me nothing. There's no pink or blue in sight. Should I ask the parents? But somehow I feel that asking the parents would be an unpardonable breach of etiquette.

I could take a chance, a fifty-fifty chance, and give the thing a male or female name. But if I'm wrong, the crowd might run me out on a rail, or stone me. They don't look like the foaming-at-the-mouth type, but adults don't have much of a sense of humor when it comes to babies.

And I can't phase out of this, because if I do, the baby will fall.

They are all waiting for me; all eyes now are on my mouth. Perhaps, since this is McGulveyland, the baby will become a male if I give it a male name, and a female if I give it a female name. That could be the reason this baby naming is so important.

What do I want it to be, a male or a female?

I can't decide—and can't help thinking that the world would be a much more relaxed place if we didn't always have to be one or the other. There would be less pressure all around. Going to a dance would be as easy as going to the drugstore.

7

Susan's father was pleasant and dignified driving them to the movies. The movie was cops and robots, starring nobody famous, and the special effects were boring. This wasn't the cops-and-robots movie Priscilla the Pill had been watching on television the other evening, it was more up-to-date, but it boiled down to pretty much the same thing. The bad guys, belonging to an international syndicate of rich people, made these killer robots with glowing eyes, because the cops had been too successful clamping down on the drug trade. After a lot of cops were lasered to death or crushed by steel arms, the police department put together a robot of their own, a more advanced, experimental model, using the brain waves of some genius cop whose entire family had been tortured to death in a way so unspeakable, the flashback didn't show all the details. The sex in the movie was provided by an heiress who fell in love with the police robot and kept trying to get him to go to bed with her. She talked dirty, had terrific legs, and in one scene showed her behind for about a second. It was stupid. Sherman put his arm around Susan, or, actually, more on the top of the back of her seat, but after a while, in that position, his arm hurt like hell. He decided to kiss her, but the movie was so awful, and she was eating popcorn, crunch-crunch-swallow, crunch-crunch-swallow, and looked so drippy in her glasses, which he had never seen before, that he thought that maybe he would put off the kissing until another time. After the movie, they waited outside for her father to come and pick them up, and Susan talked about school: who was snooty and who wasn't. They held hands. Her hand this time wasn't cold and clammy, it was warm, affectionate; it gave Sherman a feeling of being completely out of danger, as if he had arrived at a sunny haven where everything would work out and there would be no more unpleasant surprises. Susan's father told them a joke on the way home and laughed in a deep, musical voice. But Susan was annoyed with her father and spoke to him so disrespectfully, Sherman was afraid for a moment that her father might reach back and smack her in the face. He didn't remember his own father much, but remembered one time, at the breakfast table, when his father smacked Mom in the face, making her gasp and drop the cereal box. And how Mom said, with one cheek bright red, that he should please forgive her. And how for the longest time after that, no one did anything about the Rice Krispies all over the floor.

8

Hsün Hsien Wu Chang pulled me out by the hair, which hurt. At first I thought I was being translated. I was very surprised, it being much too early, by several millennia, for translation, but then, seeing my august mentor's smiling, wrinkled face, I remembered that I was Sergeant Sherm and realized that I had had a close shave to end close shaves. Underestimating myself as an enemy—that had been my mistake. Old Hsün didn't have to say a word. I hung my head, aware that for all my incredible deeds and prowess I was still a student learning lessons.

"A little humility is a good thing," he winked subliminally, "but don't wallow in it, my son." Then he winked out altogether.

So the time witches were at work here, too.

Like an actor ignoring a fluffed line, I unfurled my cape and projected my astral body up and away, back toward the House of Doors and back to Washington, to face the psi-fiend, for I was armed now with the knowledge to disarm him/her and send her/him packing, his/her tail between her/his legs. Why this asinine optionality of pronouns? My concentration was off. Disorientation, probably, from my recent imprisonment. Or interdimensional jet lag. No matter. On with the show.

Marshaling all my pneumas, personas, and noumenal umbras, I made for S Street, found S Street deserted, made for Capitol Hill—nothing there either, an occasional corpse, a severed limb—so I backtracked, half-wishing I could backtrack all the way to peaceful Invergordon (assuming it still existed). I flew down Pennsylvania Avenue toward the White House. Was I too late? The nation's capital looked like the aftermath of a plague or revolution.

Curtains drawn, windows boarded up. A solitary car in the road. The car, gutted, burnt black, lay upside down like a dead roach. This, at rush hour. The traffic lights still worked, blinking on and off in silence.

At a far intersection, by the Liberian Embassy, I saw a warted Frop brandishing a broadax, and overhead I got a glimpse, against a cloud, of one of the dragons of Cuspidor. I alighted on the White House lawn and entered the building, noting the bullet holes in the walls and the lipstick graffiti defacing the portraits of past presidents. Following the foul aura I now knew so well, I came to the Oval Office and there saw, behind a desk, Inspector Borgenicht, a stubble-jawed henchman at either elbow and an evil smirk on his lips. In his eyes there was madness.

"Poor Borgy," I murmured. "Your furniture's been rearranged."

"Poor nothing," he snorted, and yellow and green fumes came out of his nostrils. "I was a mere fifth-level magician before, albeit certified. And now—"

"And now," I said, "you are an avatar of George."

He blinked, looked at me, and said in a voice not his own, "How the hell did you know that?"

9

He took a bus to her house after school on a Friday, sat with her on the sofa in the living room for an hour listening to her talk about who was dating whom, and finally got up the nerve to kiss her. The kiss was friendly, not at all erotic, and it made Sherman feel so brimming with kindness that he kissed her again. He was very surprised at how simple and natural a thing a kiss was. Susan let him kiss her a few more times, even let him give her a kiss with a two-armed hug, chest against bosom, but she had something else she wanted to say—she had been building up to it—and brushed aside this smooching as an interruption. He and she were boyfriend and girlfriend, she said seriously, and they took a lot of things for granted. Sherman, not understanding, nodded, still in the glow of the kiss and the desire to kiss again, though Susan's mouth was not the prettiest: the upper lip stuck up too much at the top, and at one of the corners of her bottom lip she had an angry pimple with brown-gray pimple cream on it. There were some girls, Susan said, who had trouble getting dates even though they had a wonderful personality and a terrific sense of humor and were smart. It was really awful. Boys were terrible, going only by looks. Clara Davidov, for example, had worked so hard on the decorations committee for the junior prom, was a whirlwind of activity and fun, but no one, absolutely no one in her class had asked her. Susan looked Sherman in the eye. "Asked her what?" asked Sherman, feeling he was supposed to say something because of Susan's look. All he could think was: Fat Clara? "Asked her to the prom, of course," said Susan, still looking at him. And all he could think was: Who in his right mind would want to take Fat Clara to a prom? She weighed at least two hundred and fifty pounds. She looked like a truck driver. Then Sherman realized, with a horrible shiver, that Susan wanted *him* to ask Fat Clara to the junior prom. "You should ask her, Sherman," said Susan. "Do this for me." Sherman felt himself turn pale. "I'm not a junior," he said in a weak voice. "I'm only in the tenth grade." But Susan told him, warmly, squeezing his hand, that that didn't matter, there would be lots of tenth-graders there, and some seniors, too, and anyway she had talked to Clara, had a long talk with her, and Clara was expecting Sherman to call her tonight at eight to ask her to the prom. Clara had bought a dress, pink and white, at the last minute, because the prom was tomorrow. Susan gave Sherman a little kiss on the tip of his nose and said, "You're a wonderful person."

10

"I've failed," thought Professor Sherm as a lust kitten tackled him and another smothered him in her enormous bouncing twin-globe perfumed bosom. Ejaculating, cursing, he winked out. And Building C, the Yankees and the Pirates, and the whole universe came to an end, its warp and woof unraveling so completely that Planck's constant one minute equaled 6.625×10^{-27} erg seconds and the next minute 12.8 and the next minute a faded blue can of sardines.

11

When I told Sir Frank my idea, he raised his eyebrows in surprise and his mouth even fell open a little. But then he quickly recovered and said, tight-lipped, that it was crazy and would never work. "Then I'll do it without you," I said, stomping out. On the street I realized I had to go to the bathroom, so I went back—and in the corridor heard Sir Frank on the phone. He was speaking in a strange tongue. I recognized it: dragontalk. I drew my sword and kicked open the door to his room.

I had never been in Sir Frank's room before. Of all the knights, he had been the most private, not sleeping upstairs with the rest of us. Seniority, I had thought. But now my eyes were opened. A poster over his stereo showed a cloven hoof and said: SATAN RULES.

"So," I said, "you're tipping off our scaly friends."

"Fuck you," spat Sir Frank with a sneer.

With a sweep of the sword I cut the telephone cord before he had the chance to tell the dragons that now I knew that *they* knew of my plan. Sir Frank ran to an end table and pulled out a gun, but before he could raise it and shoot me, I chopped him hard in the neck. He fell, and the gun clattered out of reach. Blood spurted from the wound like a fountain, like a scene in a grisly horror movie. He glared at me.

"That's why you did all that funny Tarzan stuff," I said, "while we were fighting and dying. That's why you never killed a dragon. And that's why they set me up, that time I tried to disguise myself as one of them, and had me kill Sir Gardyloo in that phony raid. You told them, damn you." And to avenge Sir Gardyloo, Sir Mike, Sir Gawain, and the others, I ran him through a couple of times, but he was already dead, the bastard, and didn't feel it.

His blood didn't smoke or anything; it was normal red in color. So he wasn't a dragon. But why had he betrayed his own kind like this? I looked through his clothes in his chest of drawers, through some papers on his desk, found nothing interesting, but in his bed, under his pillow, there was a little black book, a diary. I opened it at random.

[ENTRY IN SIR FRANK'S DIARY]

June 7. So far so good. His attention is diverted. The hole in adventure No.9 went unnoticed. Luigi did an excellent job. V. suspects, but he can't reach us here. His turn will come. All their turns will come. Remember to bring the cordite.

[END OF ENTRY]

I took the diary with me, stepped over the lake of blood, closed the door after me, then went and packed my things. I couldn't stay in the firehouse now, of course, being the only person left. It felt haunted. I certainly wouldn't have been able to sleep there at night, not with a corpse downstairs. Even at home I needed a night-light, and if my thoughts took a certain spooky direction, I would have to turn on all my lights and turn on the radio, and sometimes I would even have to go and wake up Mom, though every minute of her sleep was more precious than gold (the car pool came by and picked her up at a quarter to seven, and she came home, on Tuesdays and Fridays, after eleven now, because of her advanced course in accounting).

12

Yipa, the African princess, was being held captive in the grass hut of the robot witch doctor from Japan. God knows what he was doing to her. Those Japanese products with their LED displays were capable of anything. They had ruined the American economy.

With great stealth I slipped down a liana, an obsidian dirk clenched in my teeth (it had a carved ebony handle: three stars and a comet), and crawled on my belly through rivermud and underbrush toward the magician's lair.

It would be an uneven fight, I knew. I had been studying magic for only a few months and still had trouble keeping the curses straight, let alone pronouncing them. As if out of spite, they all started with the letter s.

"Relax," I told myself. "Take deep breaths. Count to ten."

At about fifty yards from the grass hut, the first spell hit me, a nasty thing that made my legs come off at the knee and my arms at the elbow. The witch doctor had sensed my approach; he must have had proximity sensors. I stuck my limbs back on with a temporary anatomical glue spell, but because of my damn stutter only the left leg and the right arm took. I clenched my teeth and crawled on, leaving the rest of me for the ants.

In our jungle here the ants are worse than killer bees or piranha. An untended limb on the ground will not last more than ten minutes. This is a rough place. At night it's not wise to sleep too soundly, to stay in one position too long.

I passed a skull and recognized it at once. Mr. Stammler had given his last lecture. Good: now I didn't have to sweat the homework assignment, already more than two weeks overdue. One burden off my mind. I propped myself up on my left elbow stump so I could peer through the window of the grass hut. I saw only silhouettes. The robot seemed to be chasing Princess Yipa around a table. But maybe my eyes were playing tricks on me.

"What's the matter, Sherm?" I asked myself. "Your heart doesn't seem to be in it today."

I sighed. "I don't know," I said.

"What else do you want to do?" I asked.

"I don't know," I said.

And suddenly I felt awful; there was a sickening rush of self-pity, and I could imagine—I could see clearly—the look on Dave and Mary's faces when I walked into the gym tomorrow, all dressed up and a carnation in my lapel, with Fat Clara.

"You're a loser," I said to myself, "with your acne and blushing and stuttering. You can't get a real girl, only these ugly types that no self-respecting young male would have anything to do with. And even in your fantasies, for

Chrissake, you don't get laid, you just cream in your pants like an imbecile. That's the best you can do."

"I'm a loser," I agreed, a lump in my throat.

"And while other kids are learning things," I went on, "and joining clubs, and going on dates, and getting good in sports, you spend all your time mooning around in McGulveyland and in these stupid adventures where nothing goes right."

"They're not stupid," I said with a whine.

"Oh? When was the last time you won a battle? When was the last time you won anything? Accomplished anything? In these stupid McGulveyland adventures?"

"I have a plan," I said weakly, thinking of the helpless populace of Cuspidor. They were counting on me. If I didn't stop the dragons, who would? The air quality there was already so bad . . .

"You're a loser, Sherm. You're such a loser, you can't even be a winner in a fantasy."

With a huge lump in my throat I tossed a spell at the grass hut, making it catch on fire, and when the Japanese robot witch doctor came running out, I wove a spell to make his joints rust up. But the spell was a tongue twister and I couldn't weave it in time. The robot turned his impassive face toward me and with a high-speed megabyte spell made my penis and testicles fall off. Everyone laughed, even the princess, when they rolled down my left trouser leg and plopped into the mud.

13

Lately, Old Corduroy has been giving me history lessons. They're not real history lessons, of course, with dates and names of kings, and he doesn't stand and lec-

ture. We go for walks and he points out objects of interest
and makes a remark or two, often enigmatic. I'll ask a
question, and he'll give me an answer that may explain
something or may not.

Most of McGulveyland, once, was under water. For this
reason, on some mountain peaks, particularly in the south,
you occasionally find coral growing or might step on an
eel.

There was an ice age here, too, with huge glaciers and
woolly mammoths. But fortunately it lasted only about a
week.

There are no fossils in McGulveyland. Old Corduroy
doesn't even understand the concept. He rubs his nose
and giggles.

The national sport has always been marbles. Old Corduroy showed me a shooter carbon-dated at two-point-five
million years. It's in a museum under a tiny bell jar filled
with argon, and the guards don't like you to stand too
close.

There has been no religious persecution here. No religious wars. And I've seen no sign of racial prejudice, even
though there are more races and species among the citizens of McGulveyland than grains of sand on the seashore.

No taxes, as has already been mentioned—to wit, the
theory that Mr. McGulvey came here to avoid them.

No death.

If someone falls under the wheels of a train, paramedics
come very quickly and use a couple of anatomical glue
spells, and after a transfusion or two the person may be a
little shaken but is none the worse for the experience. As
good as new. An acquaintance of mine, a dwarfish, nut-
brown individual originally from Sri Lanka, who lives in
the trunk of an old banyan tree and is always smoking a
large calabash pipe (the bowl is almost as big as his head),

claims he once fell by accident into a tree-limb shredder and was cut into more than a hundred pieces. As proof he shows me a hospital bill, itemized. He smiles, hands me a magnifying glass, and asks me to find a scar on him. I look carefully, closely, at his forehead, chin, hands, a calf and knee (he lifts his trouser leg), but as far as I can see, the skin is unbroken. Not a seam anywhere. Nothing resembling a zipperlike stitch. So apparently medicine in McGulveyland is quite advanced, despite its reliance on what you and I would call astrology.

Old Corduroy takes me to a field, an ordinary-looking field, and in the middle of it points at the ground. Not far from our feet is a wet patch, where the grass and weeds are half in water. Then I see that it's not water but a kind of low mist, semitransparent, and below the mist is a picture of a street and houses. I bend over—Old Corduroy with gestures cautions me not to step on the patch itself—and I look hard. I would almost swear that I'm looking, from above, at a block in some suburb in reality. I can't make out the street signs or the license plates on the cars in the driveways, but the conviction grows in me that this is a view of none other than Penn Hills, where I live.

I see movement: a kid on a bicycle. Then a car passes. I hear a dog bark. Only an image? Or . . .

"What is this?" I ask Old Corduroy.

"It's a hole," he says.

I understand. McGulveyland, wonderful as it is, is not perfect. There are a few holes in it.

And so there must be more prosaic ways of getting here than by phasing. If you knew the right place, you could put a ladder on your roof and climb up into this field. Then pull the ladder up after you, to avoid attracting attention.

"Do a lot of people come here from reality?" I ask Old Corduroy.

He shrugs. "Not really."

"Does anyone here ever fall through a hole?" I ask, imagining one of the Slob Brothers landing on somebody's lawn, twenty feet tall, with a bushy black beard and a club that makes a caveman's club look like a toothpick.

"Hardly ever," replies Old Corduroy. He's fidgeting, taking his yo-yo out of his pocket and putting it back in. He probably wants to go on to something else. Short attention span. "Nancy Collins fell through. But that was before your time. McGulvey finally had to go and get her back."

"You mean," I say, "that Mr. McGulvey went to reality?"

"Sure."

"When was this? A couple of years ago?"

"More."

"Ten years ago?"

Old Corduroy shrugs. He doesn't know. It could have been ten years ago, it could have been in the eighteenth century, Earth time. It's hard to tell, here.

I ask questions about Nancy Collins. Old Corduroy is tired of the subject. The simplest thing is to take me to Nancy Collins herself, which he does. By coincidence (or it's not coincidence) she lives only a few minutes away, in an apartment house overlooking the bazaar.

I knock, and a plump lady opens the door. She looks very dignified and wealthy, like someone at an opera, but instead of holding a lorgnette she's holding a goofy trumpet-nosed dinker, and her dress is striped like an awning. The colors of the stripes are lime ice cream and supersonic red. It makes my eyes swim.

"Mrs. Collins?" I ask.

"I gave at the office," she says pleasantly but firmly.

I explain, as Old Corduory squirms and sighs a deep sigh of boredom, that I'm interested in her otherworldly accident.

"Oh," she says. "It was dreadful. I couldn't speak a word of their language."

"What language was that?"

"Chinese, I think."

"And Mr. McGulvey came and saved you?"

She brightened; she positively glowed. "He's a wonderful man."

Chapter Six

• 1 •

Whitney High School in gray-tan letters on the brick over the entrance. Cracks in the sidewalk, in places so wide, little bushes are growing in them, making kids trip when they come running from the bus in the morning or to the bus (a hell of a lot faster) when the bell rings at 3:15. Overhead, in a pale blue sky, a flying saucer-runabout briefly flicks. No one notices, because no one happens to be looking up.

Mr. Bromberg and Mr. Hollis will be in charge of security tonight at the junior prom, standing at the entrance to collar gate-crashers, keep an eye out (and sniff) for signs of alcohol consumption, and discourage vandalism in the parking lot. Some kinds of disruption, however, come from within. Against these, security guards are powerless.

For example, three trays of cookies are missing. The cafeteria person, Mrs. Kirchstein, and the potbellied custodian, Harry, are having fifty fits. The principal, Mr. Bartlett, when he was informed, knitted his hedgehog eyebrows and sent out an order to the doughnut shop across the street, to replace the filched refreshments. Under his breath he is muttering four-letter words. If he had his way, there would be not only corporal punishment in the schools, there would be, yes, damn it, capital punishment. A firing squad, behind the tennis court, for repeated offenders. Up against the wall with those unregenerate scuzzballs who persist in taking his gas cap and breaking off his aerial. It would be no loss, I can tell you. They will never make a contribution to society.

The gym is being prepared: streamers, chains of construction paper, balloons, glue and glitter on cutout letters. On a stepladder, Fat Clara, flushed. Long straw-yellow hair hangs across her large forehead, across her twinkling eyes. She is her usual cheerful, wisecracking self, and her friends on the decorations committee have no inkling of the recent triumph in her life, just as they had no inkling, before, of the defeat that made her cry for hours into her pink-flowered pillow.

2

Sherman had a long, rotten day. He did a load of laundry in the morning, took Terhune out in the cold rain to squat, scribbled down some last-minute overdue English homework (stupid participial phrases), and after school escorted Priscilla the Pill home from her bus stop, still in the cold rain. Then he had to go to the market for milk and bread, and then clean the toilet, which smelled twice as awful as usual because of the humidity. At supper Mom yelled at him because she had a headache and something was going wrong at work again. Her yelling rang in his ears too much for him to phase to McGulveyland in his room after supper. He got into a fight with Priscilla the Pill, and didn't even have the satisfaction of getting in a good punch—his timing was off—between her bite and his punishment from Mom of more yelling and no movies for a month. Then he had to call Fat Clara at eight and go through that whole torture again. Mrs. Davidov told him, after letting him guh-guh-guh like a cretin for five or ten minutes, that Clara was doing emergency baby-sitting at the Johnsons and he should call her there. The Johnsons were around the corner, so he walked over—he couldn't face the phone again—and Fat Clara made him hold one of the twins while she changed the other, and it cheesed all over his shoulder. "Hurt yourself?" she asked, seeing the Band-Aid on his thumb. "My sister bit me," he said. "She'll grow out of it," Fat Clara said, putting twin number 1 in the crib and taking twin number 2, who now also had a load. "Mr. Gillespie—Barry's father—will pick us up tomorrow. He's one of the chaperones," she went on. "And for my corsage, it should be a white carnation and a wrist one." Fat Clara put down twin number 2, cleaned off Sherman's shoulder (but it still smelled), and led him to the Johnsons' kitchen, where she made him cocoa and told him that she planned to be a nurse and was already working as a candy striper at the hospital because of her kid brother's leukemia. Sherman did not know about her kid brother's leukemia, did not even know she had a kid brother, so he mumbled an apology. Fat Clara told him about Mr. Schaub, who was too vain to wear his glasses and couldn't find the chalk half the time; about Louise, who hadn't come back after the spring vacation because she was pregnant and her parents took her to California to have the baby and put it up for adoption there; and about what Mary had spent on her prom dress—more than two hundred dollars, even though her father was out of work. Sherman, watching Fat Clara's mouth as she talked, thought that never in a million years would he be able to bring himself to kiss her after a date, she was so big and ugly. She had the mouth of a man. The chin of a man. The shoulders of a man. Sherman dreaded tomorrow. Everyone would laugh at him. "You and I are a lot alike," she said, looking him in the face, "even though you're shy and I'm not. We're both deep. We both have private lives that nobody knows about."

3

My plan had been to have the mayor declare a Clean Up Cuspidor Day and stage an event—say, collecting litter in the park by the zoo. This would lure the dragons out, tempting them to an act of malicious, mocking sabotage. I would set a trap for them, a booby trap—planting dynamite, say, in the foundations of the skyscraper directly north of the park, so that the building would fall and squash them all flat. Of course, the building and the adjacent buildings would have to be evacuated first—quietly, surreptitiously—and realistic dummies would have to be placed at various windows, to keep the dragons from suspecting anything. The strength of the idea, I felt, was its unsubtlety. The enemy, ever devious and deceitful, would not be prepared for so crude a blow—the use of an entire office building as a club.

True, the citizens collecting litter in the park (our decoys, so to speak) would be squashed flat as well. Yet wasn't that an acceptable sacrifice—their lives, in addition to the cost, not negligible, of the building—when you considered that the city itself had its back to the wall environmentally? These people would die anyway, along with everyone else in Cuspidor, but slowly and horribly, if we didn't do something.

Except now, thanks to Sir Frank, cursed be his memory, the dragons knew of my plan. And they knew that I knew that they knew. The way the telephone connection had been broken after Sir Frank's snarl of surprise. I frowned, then thought carefully. If they knew that I knew that they knew, then they would be expecting me to change my plan. I would fool them, outclever them: I would *not* change it.

I got into Sir Frank's car—a Toyota, automatic—and drove to City Hall. Without incident, though there was a lot of traffic and drivers with short tempers. I double-parked in a towaway zone. Let them tow it, I didn't care. The showdown was approaching, the denouement, the last page of this adventure. My heart beat faster.

The mayor wasn't in. I took the elevator up to the seventh floor, the Department of Health. The director was in. No tinge of green on this man; human through and through, he shook my hand. He had great respect, he said, for what we knights were trying to do.

I told him my idea, but decided to leave out the part about the booby trap and dynamiting office buildings. Civil servants were not original thinkers—he would probably balk at the dynamite. It didn't matter, I could take care of that end of it myself. Too bad, though, about the people in the building, because now, since I would be doing this privately, there was no way to evacuate them. More martyrs to the cause. Hundreds more, maybe even a few thousand. But this was no time to count heads. We had a job to do.

The dragons hadn't pulled their punches. Why should we?

The director thought the Clean Up Cuspidor Day idea was brilliant and shook my hand again, beaming with admiration and gratitude. "We'll start a publicity campaign on this, first thing," he said. "There are many people out there, more than you imagine, who are tired of what's been happening to our city."

Outside, the Toyota hadn't been towed, but there was a pink-and-white ticket under the windshield wiper. With a smile I began to tear up the ticket.

But my smile faded when I read, on the ticket I was tearing in half, not "Cuspidor" but "District of Columbia." In panic, I looked around, afraid I would see the Washington Monument or the Capitol in the distance. I didn't.

Relieved, I got in, put the psi-fiend out of my mind, and went to buy fuses and plunger-detonators.

4

Sidestepping a blast of raw psi, I removed Old Borgy's head—regretfully, but my friend was gone in any case, gone like a candle snuffed out, like a lamp turned off—and with his head (its teeth still clicking) I bowled over the two stubble-jawed henchmen. A split, a difficult spare, but no problem for Sergeant Sherm. But then Borodin, the chemist turned arch-evil in this time line because he had been distracted from his pursuit of music by the buttocks of a woman from the Upper Devonian, stepped from behind a marble column and threw vitriol in my face before I could shield myself physically or otherwise, and I was blinded. This blindness, I knew at once, was irreversible and permanent. From here on out, I would have to rely exclusively on my second sight, which was spotty at best, intermittent, and there was no Hsün Hsien Wu Chang to fall back on now. It didn't look good, even with my plan. It didn't look good. And the pain was indescribable.

5

V. Snerk returns from his cousin's in Barnett-by-the-Gulf with a bad sunburn. His bald head is cranberry red.

"Is there anything I can do for you, V.?" I ask feebly, shocked to see him ill. A physician should never be ill. (And there should be no illness, anyway, in McGulveyland.) "One of your poultices, perhaps? You can tell me how."

He sighs, gets into bed, and pulls the covers up to his neck, the counterpane with long, awkward storks on it. I sit near him, not knowing what to do. I don't think I have ever been this unhappy outside reality.

From the library, a stink, faint but unmistakable, of lemon feces. My time here is limited; that's what the stink is telling me. And V.'s hands—I can see them—are trembling.

"Can I get you a glass of water?" I ask. I'm so upset, the words don't even come out. Instead, I make a stupid sound, like a sheep.

V. smiles a little smile, to show me that things are not all that bad and I shouldn't worry too much, but it's plain that he's so ill now that he can't even talk. I hold his hand.

I should do something. Find Mr. McGulvey. V. may have a temperature. He's gone from cranberry red to beet red and getting darker. Lord knows what his physiology is like—he may not even have a liver—but this certainly doesn't look good. It doesn't look good at all.

6

The tuxedo and the corsage he got with Larry Carson's help. Larry was a senior with three proms already under his belt. He was going to a fancy college in New England to study law. He had money. Being a friend of Dave's, he agreed to give Sherman a hand. (Dave knew all sorts of people, even guys who had dropped out of high school years ago. They had hard-bitten faces, tattoos on their arms, were married, and there was always car grease under their fingernails.) "Keep everything together," Larry told Sherman. "Suspenders, shoes. Put it all in a bag when you're done. If one cuff link is missing, they charge you fifty dollars." Mom didn't yell about the rental, oddly enough, or even grumble; she gave Sherman a look, as if he had announced that he was royalty and she was not completely sure that he was lying or crazy because there was an outside chance it might be true. Priscilla the Pill asked who the girl was. Sherman replied with a long look of hate, then said, "None of your business" through clenched teeth. But Priscilla the Pill smiled smugly and said she would find out sooner or later, because her friend Rita's older sister was going. Sherman realized then, with a shiver, that he would have to kill his sister. The time had come. Susan called and talked about dresses and what colors went with what colors, and what a good deed Sherman was doing. She said she would want a detailed account of the prom on Sunday. A horn honked in the street. It was Mr. Gillespie. In the car were Barry, a girl Sherman didn't know—Barry's date, a blonde—and Fat Clara, in her prom dress, looking twice as big and more like a truck driver than ever. There was hardly room to sit; he had to squeeze in, and endure being pressed into the door handle by a mountain of perfumed flesh that was too warm. "It's not her fault," Sherman thought. He remembered, in elementary school, a girl called Beth who was ugly as sin, talked drunkenly because she was tongue-tied, and drooled a lot. She may have been hunchbacked, too;

she was always stooped over. But Beth had won the spring spelling bee, had come in first in the school, struggling and stumbling over every letter but getting, incredibly, every letter right. And the whole class applauded at the end, even though Beth was such a pathetic ugly duckling with her frizzy hair and her stooping and drooling.

7

My plan, based on what I had learned in dimension X, on the planet Here, as a giant slug, was to—

But what treachery was this? From the head of my departed friend, Inspector Borgenicht, emerged unexpectedly a tongue—no, it was too long and sinuous for a tongue. I focused my second sight (all the sight I had now, alas), and saw it was a snake, a venomous reptile with eyes like embers. It made for me with a speed beyond that of any snake, for it came like a wild boar, like a diesel train in the night, like a missile intent on the radioactive vaporization of a city filled with innocent men, women, and children.

I threw up a parrying spell, but behind me—

A warted Frop, swinging a poleax, and—

Benjamin Harrison, his wig awry, on all fours, turned rabid beast, biting my ankle—

And therefore, distracted, I was unprepared for—

Argh.

Sergeant Sherm oh no gets re, rearran. Reargh. Ranged. My furn. Ni. Ture.

George.

It took only a second. It was very easy. Everything on this we-world was very easy. That's what set my teeth on edge (figuratively speaking, because I didn't have teeth; slugs don't have teeth). When life is too easy, it makes a fellow want to punch the most valuables. Things, people. Sledgehammer Tiffany lamps. Machine-gun big holes, pop-pop-pop, into hand-waving, open-mouthed bodies. No resistance. Like soft butter. Driving me crazy.

In a frenzy, I picked up a poleax, to chop this revoltingly we-wimpy city to the ground. But then the poleax wasn't there. And—what was this?—the city was all different. The buildings were a lot taller, a lot grayer. They switched cities on me? Someone playing a joke? Or was this another gosh-darn fault? These gosh-darn faults weren't supposed to happen so gosh-darn often. At this rate, I might not—shudder—make it to translation. Too many indeterminates for a fellow to trip over.

The air was dirty, full of compounds of sulfur and hydrocarbons. The sign said WELCOME TO CUSPIDOR. With a growl I kicked over the sign and advanced, sucking up nearby souls and spitting them out: yuck, the taste just as namby-pamby here. I hummed with blood lust, murder, mayhem.

8

Mrs. Decowski was there, talking to Mr. Stammler. (They were probably talking about the American Constitution.) Parents were there, too, all uncomfortable: some shifted from foot to foot and kept averting their eyes, and some were embarrassingly loud. Sherman looked around, but didn't see Dave or Mary. Thank God. Fat Clara took him by the arm and led him to one group of people after another. People shook his hand as if they knew him, though no one had ever seen him before. Sherman hadn't participated in any school activities, hadn't gone to any of the baseball or basketball or football games after school.

"Who is that?" was written on everyone's face. But Fat Clara not only didn't mind, she smirked to herself, as if the whole thing was a wonderful joke. Sherman, too, began to see the humor of it. He joined Fat Clara in smirking secretly at these good-looking, hair-in-place, most-likely-to-succeed types.

The first shock Sherman received that evening was at the punch bowl, after Fat Clara left him to go to the bathroom with several other girls in rustling dresses and wrist corsages. Looking to his left, where there was an odd momentary absence of noise, he almost dropped his cup of punch. It was Princess Martha Anne herself, standing right next to him and giving him the fisheye.

Was she angry with him because of that recent business with the Frops? It was hard to tell with Princess Martha Anne. He was going to stammer something—anything—when the full significance of this encounter hit home. First there had been the contamination of the library, then the contamination of the adventures, then the discovery that McGulveyland had holes . . . and now reality itself, it seemed, was being invaded. What if the psi-fiend came here, what if it showed up tonight at the junior prom?

Unthinkable.

Or a naked time witch?

Unthinkable.

Sherman broke into a cold sweat. "I must be dreaming," he thought, though he knew he wasn't. He took another look at Princess Martha Anne, hoping that maybe in his overwrought state his eyes had deceived him. That this person, a Whitney High School junior or senior, simply bore a striking resemblance to the warrior princess who had pulled him and Sir Gardyloo out of so many jams in the past.

Mr. Bartlett walked by, smiled and nodded at Sherman,

and walked on, to smile and nod at the other students along his path, making sure that everything was going smoothly. The disappearance of the cookies had put the principal on his guard, and he saw villainy lurking everywhere, villainy ready to jump out any minute, rear its ugly head, and run amok.

"Care for some punch?" Sherman said to Princess Martha Anne. He ladled a cup of the frothy pink stuff for her, and his hand didn't shake as badly as it might have.

"Cover your rear," was all she said, taking the cup, and in the next moment had melted into the crowd.

One of the parents, a father, smiled in Sherman's direction. He was short, stout, mostly bald, and had a red goatee. A red goatee? Sherman looked hard at him. The man winked. It was—no question about it—bold as brass after his treachery, Arnie MacTavish.

9

The magician has a red goatee, too, and on his peaked cap are three stars and a comet. His eyebrows are not red but white with a blue tinge; they don't go with the MacTavish goatee at all. My fantasy life is going downhill, I realize, going to the dogs, and even as I think dogs, Terhune lumbers out awkwardly from behind the magician's robe and wags his tail once, twice. It used to whish like a whip, that tail. I pat my old friend's head sadly. He looks up at me, as if to say, "Wasn't this clever of me? Aren't you glad I'm here?"

When I tell the magician the problem with V., he nods and rests his chin on his fist. (The goatee is gone now. It doesn't matter.) Then he plucks his lower lip. "Poultice," he mutters. "Jupiter." Apparently, he is an alumnus of the same school as V.

He invites me in. A large apartment with a sliding glass door that leads to a terrace overlooking a pond and a playground. The magician is comfortably off.

"Barry," he says, holding out his hand, introducing himself.

I shake his hand, surprised. He is much younger than I thought. But before I can look at his eyebrows again, to check their color, my attention is drawn to the jigsaw puzzles on the floor. I had taken them for carpets. They're enormous, beautiful, the kind with tens of thousands of pieces.

The most I ever tried was a five-thousander, and it took forever just to get the frame completed. The puzzle almost filled up the Ping-Pong table in the basement. Then pieces got lost when Terhune thumped against the table once, or Priscilla the Pill swept her coat over it for no reason, just to be nasty. The light's no good down there, but Mom said the dining room table was out of the question. Even though we never eat in the dining room and the wood of that table is smooth and unbroken. (It has only one scratch, long but not very deep, and that wasn't my fault.) The Ping-Pong table is awful in the middle, where the two halves come together—or, rather, won't come together, no matter what you do.

But here in the magician's apartment there is plenty of light, from the terrace, and the floor is wonderful, a glossy warm parquet whose color, tan-gold, reminds me of circus sawdust. One puzzle is a Bavarian castle in winter, incredibly tall and intricate; and there's a New England barn and field in autumn; and a Mediterranean coastal resort with deck chairs and multicolored flags under a tangerine sun.

While I wait, the magician disappears with a pop, hold-

ing his hat so it won't blow off in transit, to examine V. I
tell Terhune to sit, afraid he might step on a puzzle.
Terhune sits. With another pop the magician reappears.
Now his face is tired, wrinkled, as if he was up all night
doing his income tax. Gently he leads me out to the
terrace, where he tells me—as I watch little children
playing on the swings below—that he's afraid V. has
leukemia.

10

I planted the dynamite in all the necessary basements.
For the dynamite I had to sell Sir Mike's set of weights
and weight-lifting bench and Sir Bob's stereo equipment.
They wouldn't be needing these things in whatever happy
hunting ground it was or valley of shadows they now
inhabited, but I felt guilty, because I could picture Sir
Mike hefting the barbells with that good-natured grin of
his, which even the grimacing, the grunting, and the
standing out of the veins in his neck couldn't erase. And I
could picture Sir Bob lying back on his bunk with his
earphones on and eyes closed, his lips moving to the
words of some song only he knew and heard. Would I
ever see them again? I wouldn't. They were gone forever.
I had the feeling that not only was this story drawing to its
conclusion, but that everything was concluding on me, the
magic library and McGulveyland, too, and that soon there
would be no more purple-heather mountaintop, precipice,
and lilac mist to go to, and I would be stuck forever with
Priscilla the Pill at the bus stop, my comic book collection
my only amusement. But that was concluding on me, too,
because even my favorite numbers now—old Flashes, old
Spidermans and Daredevils, and two really ancient Cap-

tain Marvels—were like chewing gum in your mouth after you've been chewing for three hours straight at a double feature. My heart wasn't in it, but I planted the dynamite anyway and ran all the cords to the master plunger-detonator, which I hid in a janitor's closet behind a bunch of mops.

A momentary distraction: I was pulled back to the Whitney High School junior prom by shrill screaming from the girls' bathroom. It echoed down the hall and reached us in the gym, even over the loud music and all the talking. Something serious must have happened to make them scream like that. I went into the hall, looked, and caught a glimpse of a gorilla running. It was being chased by Barbara Shoemaker, who was on the girls' basketball team and almost as big as Fat Clara. Furious, she was trying to hit the animal with her beaded purse, which she swung from a long black strap as if it were a mace on a chain. (I forget what those mace-on-chain things are called in medieval battles.) The gorilla ran, holding its hands up to protect its head, and didn't seem to know how to get out of the building; it would keep stopping and looking around for a door, but of course all the classroom doors were locked in the evening, and that let Barbara catch up to it—she was fast, even in her prom dress—and whack it again with her beaded purse. When the gorilla stopped and looked in my direction, I saw it wasn't a gorilla at all but Gfarf. Mr. Bartlett hurried past me, just as furious as Barbara Shoemaker, his hands extended, ready to clutch and apprehend. The ridiculous thought occurred to me that Gfarf might be suspended for this. But of course it wasn't his fault. The fault was all the gosh-darn faults spreading like cracks in an eggshell, making characters slip from book to book, from world to world, and putting the psi-fiend now in Cuspidor. Speaking of which, I had to get back to my dynamite and Clean Up Cuspidor Day in the park, to trap the dragons and exterminate them root and branch.

11

"Some weird pervert creep in the ladies' room," Fat Clara told me, returning, flushed and pleased, as if the incident had been part of the entertainment and had gone off successfully. "He had a club, too, like Alley Oop."

Mr. Hollis and Mr. Bromberg, with an off-duty policeman, were on the scene now, but Mr. Bartlett, using his bullhorn take-charge voice, made everyone leave the hall and go back into the gym, so I couldn't see what happened next.

Dave tapped me on the shoulder.

"Hey, Sherman," he said, "I hear your date is Fat Clara."

I almost fainted, I was so mortified.

She, fortunately, was out of earshot, arranging something by a table with a couple of other students and a mother.

Dave grinned at me with a grin that would have gone through three inches of lead.

It was the kind of grin that you can never forget, the kind that makes you writhe thirty years later.

With this awful grin, he whispered something to me. About kissing, about me and Fat Clara. I didn't really hear it, because I was so mortified.

Fat Clara came back and took me by the hand to lead me to another activity, which turned out to be dancing. I knew I would look comical dancing with her—she was almost a foot taller than me and more than twice as wide—

but I noticed the delicate way she held out her hand, the one I was supposed to hold as we danced, the hand with the wrist corsage. I understood then that even if on the outside she looked like a truck driver, on the inside she wanted to be a woman, like other girls, and that she had a right to.

"What's the matter, Sherm?" she asked. "You look like you were hit by a truck."

I was stunned.

"How—why did you call me Sherm?" I asked.

"A nickname for Sherman. You don't like it?"

She was so natural, so much at home, so straightforward. I decided that I shouldn't call her—I shouldn't even think of her as—Fat Clara. Just Clara. As if she were a normal person.

"It's all right," I said.

"You're red as a beet."

"They call me Red Light," I told her, trying to laugh.

"Sherman is sort of nerdy, I think. Sherm is worlds better. Someone made a remark, didn't they? I know. I get that all the time, behind my back. That's my life. They call you Red Light? They call me Fat Clara." She smiled at me. "It's not easy being fat and ugly when you're a girl."

"You're not fat and ugly," I said, almost choking.

"I appreciate your taking me to the prom, Sherm. I was on the committee, you know, and it would have been *terrible* if no one asked me."

"You're okay," I said, and looked her in the face, eye to eye, angrily, ready to yell at her, really yell at her, if she said she wasn't.

12

Mr. McGulvey wasn't around. The house was empty, no one dropped by, and the sky was a heavy, achy gray, as if there was going to be a cold rain, the kind that lasts all day. Sherman thought that maybe he should just phase back home and do Mr. Stammler's homework, get it out of the way for a change instead of saving it for the last minute.

Susan had sat him down on the sofa after lunch today, when he went over there, as he was supposed to, and had asked him for his report on the junior prom. Who did what, who wore what, and what were the comments, and was Fat Clara happy. He wasn't good at supplying information—he was retarded when it came to remembering dresses and comments—but Susan wasn't annoyed with him, having heard everything from three or four people already. She beamed, put her arms around him, and gave him a kiss, but quickly, because her mother was in the kitchen rattling pots and pans. It was okay with Sherman that the kiss was quick. He didn't like it. He realized that he didn't like Susan. She was stuck-up, pushy, though that hadn't been apparent at first. Some faults didn't show themselves at first.

Heaving a sigh, he left the porch and went to the library. Would the library, in time, be able to purge itself of *Lust Kittens*? It had been around, after all, for thousands of years (at least) and should know how to take a little human sin in stride.

13

So, having planted the dynamite in the basement of the big office building directly north of the municipal park, and having run all the cords to the master plunger-detonator hidden behind a bunch of mops in a janitor's closet on the second floor, I get little Billy LoBianco, with his freckles and missing front teeth, to stand in the closet with a luminous-dial countdown stopwatch. At the appointed time today, noon, he will depress the plunger. He'll be blown up with the building, of course, since he's only on the second floor, not that far from the charges. But I don't have time—or the know-how—to set up a shortwave radio-activated switch, the kind one has on one's garage door if one is as well-off as the Simpsons down the block. Anyway, little Billy is already dead—or at death's door, from slow starvation—in another adventure. If you can call these stupid stories "adventures." I'm in a bad mood, I guess, because of the prom. A quick death will put him mercifully out of his misery, if he's still alive. And if he's not alive, it doesn't matter, then, does it? You can't kill someone who's already been killed. I brush the boy's sandy hair with my hand and tell him to be sure to depress the plunger on the dot, not a second before, not a second after; timing is everything. I tell him that the City of Cuspidor will be eternally grateful for his heroism today. He seems nervous—not because of the dynamite, which he doesn't understand, but because of the closet. It's dark when the door is closed. I tell him to look at the luminous dial and think about a big cake made of *lakol*. I promise him that if all goes well—and I'm sure it will—I'll take him fishing in the Pickle, and we'll catch a mess of squeak-fish and make a musical bracelet out of them for his hardworking mother.

14

Mom, out of the blue, said to Sherm, while he was trying to fix the Ping-Pong table in the basement, that they ought to have a talk.

"I know I've been wrought-up lately," she said, holding the laundry basket, propping it on her hip. "There's been a lot going on. At the office. My evening course. The car repairs."

It seemed extremely peculiar to Sherm that it was in their dim, dank, mildewy, and sewage-smelly basement that Mom was choosing to have one of her extremely rare human-to-human explanations with him.

"I know I've been yelling a lot."

Sherm shrugged, feeling embarrassed for her sake.

"Of course, you've been difficult," she went on. "Fighting with your sister. You're a little old for that. Sixteen. And the way you moon around, not all there. Deaf half the time."

Sherm didn't feel like sixteen. He didn't even feel like a teenager. Maybe nine, ten, eleven.

"It's difficult," Mom went on, "bringing up a teenage son without a father."

Fathers were not such a bargain, Sherm thought. Look at Pete Russo with his horror stories in the cafeteria, and his long-drawn-out, wouldn't-it-be-wonderful plots of murdering the Old Man. The vat of acid. The rain of bricks from a private plane. The burial up to the chin in the desert of Death Valley with molasses smeared all over the head to bring the fire ants.

"Teenage boys," Mom said, "need a father figure."

"Authority," she said.

"Some discipline," she said.

Christ, thought Sherm, is she thinking of marrying a Marine sergeant?

"Next weekend, Saturday," Mom said, coming closer, her face filled with lines, "I'd like you to be home. I know you have a girlfriend. That's fine. But next Saturday, Sherman, for the afternoon and dinner, I'd like you to be home. Please, for me. I'd like you to meet someone."

Sherm took Terhune to the lot, his thoughts at such loose ends after this bombshell that he stepped in a big wet turdpile, and it took half an hour, using sticks and an old toothbrush, to get the stuff out of the treads of his sneakers.

15

Clean Up Cuspidor Day. This is it, the showdown. The director of health is on the bandstand, at the microphone, with other officials, and they're shaking each other's hands and giving each other certificates of appreciation or plaques for service, while citizens of this fair city—this foul city— are lining up to receive big bright-yellow litterbags that say CLEAN UP CUSPIDOR. There's another line for those long sticks with nails on the end of them that you use to skewer trash without having to bend over. And there's a table full of paper cups—bright yellow, saying CLEAN UP CUSPIDOR— containing not soda, which is bad for your teeth, complexion, and heart, but apple juice that has no additives, one hundred percent pure, or spring water bottled in a province far from cities and automobiles. A sunny day, a pleasant breeze, streamers, refreshments, smiles.

The dragons will strike. They have to. Even if they smell a trap, this is just too much of a provocation for them to resist. My eyes search the sky as the director of health puts his arm around me and says laudatory things about the valiant knights who daily put their lives on the line, etc. He is about to launch into some ceremony—I'm listening with half an ear—they want to present me with a parchment diploma and a loving cup—but, looking at my watch, I apologize and excuse myself. There are only a few minutes to go, and naturally I want to get the hell out of the park before the office building to the north, that massive monolith, comes down on everything here like a marble lid on a tomb. The director of health is chagrined; he must have gone to considerable trouble to prepare this presentation, he must have a few speeches more to deliver, and the photographers are lined up, waiting for their cue. But there's really no point in being polite, I tell myself. The director may have hurt feelings now, but in a few minutes he'll be squashed flat as a bug on a windshield, so it doesn't matter, does it?

Where are the damned dragons? It's almost time. Muttering, looking up, looking again at my watch, I leave the bandstand, pulling myself away from the director's arm and the officials' hands outstretched to shake mine. They practically throw the loving cup at me as I go down the steps—so at least I'll have that. It's huge, golden, heavy, with two handles and swirling curlicue letters that read: FROM THE GRATEFUL CITIZENS OF CUSPIDOR, TO SIR SHERM, FOR HIS UNFLAGGING—I don't have time to read the rest of the inscription, I'm half-running through the crowd, which is surprisingly dense. The turnout is much greater than anyone expected. A lot of people, evidently, have had it up to here with this pollution. The cleanup is an idea whose time has come.

The sky is clear—almost blue, in fact, as if to mock me, saying, "See? The pollution wasn't really all that bad." And the knife-twisting thought occurs to me that a Clean Up Cuspidor Day might have worked just fine without the dynamite: because when people get mobilized, when they finally shake off their apathy, then even conspiracies of dragons from another planet can't stop them. As I run, banging into people with my loving cup, glancing nervously at my watch, at the sky—nothing, not a speck of a silhouette of a dragon, and there's less than a minute now to go, forty seconds, thirty-five seconds—as I run, another thought occurs to me, even more knife-twisting than the last thought, and the last thought still stings: What if the dragons don't show up on purpose? What if they're waiting for me to blow up the building first? And then they'll show up, laughing at me, getting the last laugh. . . . They always get the last laugh, curse them.

In a panic, I charge through the crowd of citizens. There are so many people. As if the whole city is showing up today to clean up Cuspidor. They're pouring into the park from all directions. A lady frowns at me; a man, who looks a lot like the late Louis Stack (five *l*'s in that last phrase), asks me what my big hurry is. "Excuse me, sorry," I say, breathless, stepping on people's feet, knocking them aside with my enormous trophy. Why am I holding on to it? Why don't I just drop the damned thing? Twenty seconds, fifteen seconds . . . I don't drop it, I realize, for the reason that I never received a trophy before, a gold loving cup. Having never been in sports in school. Never on a bowling team. And even if I had been, I wouldn't have won anything. My strikes are dumb luck, and I never get spares.

Zero hour. With the loving cup from the grateful citizens of Cuspidor I squeeze through one of the gates, past a fat man with a pot belly who reminds me of our custodian, Harry, and I look back and see that the park is packed with smiling people and bright-yellow CLEAN UP CUSPIDOR bags. From the bandstand the director of health looks in my direction reproachfully. A beautiful, festive day, not a dragon in sight, as the explosion—on the dot—roars, grows, and the office building sweeps the park with its shadow, like a low passing plane, as it slowly falls.

An uncontrollable fit of giggling. It *is* comic, in a way, if you look at it objectively, what a sap I made of myself trying to outclever the dragons, ending up killing all these innocent people for nothing. My giggling stops when I see a hand flying through the air. It's a small hand, torn red tatters of flesh at the wrist. It's Billy LoBianco's hand. He did his job well, poor little kid. At least, I tell myself, his end was quick, not lingering. The hand—probably the very hand that depressed the plunger—lands in the chainlink fence in front of me, and it doesn't bounce off, it clings to the mesh of the fence, because the slightly curved fingers catch on the wires. A good thing, I tell myself, that little Billy's mother isn't here to see this. She would probably faint dead away at the sight. And it must be tough (I also think) for Mrs. Davidov, with her elementary-school son having leukemia, and everyone trying to stay cheerful for months, maybe even years, while they wait for his death.

There's a big thud and a whoosh as the building hits the park like the slap of a giant, squashing God knows how many folk into a pulp whose description you'd rather not think about. A cloud of brick-and-concrete dust, a whirlwind of leaves from splintered trees, a few more roars and whooshes as things collapse and settle and subside, and then it's over. Silence. No sirens, no people groaning or calling for help. I look up and, sure enough, here come the dragons. They're too far for me to see their faces, but I know that every one of those green bastards is grinning. I'm not in their league, that's for sure. I feel like fifty idiots rolled into one, standing here holding this huge loving cup from the grateful citizens of Cuspidor for my unflagging—

The dragons—there are hundreds of them now, all flapping their devil-wings above the park, which is sealed shut by a mammoth gravestone that has endless rows and columns of blown-in or blown-out windows—the dragons are gathering to have this tremendous last laugh at me, who tried so hard and persistently to discomfit them in the past, to defeat them, to expel them. Their laughter, as they hover in the air between the buildings, becomes diabolical music played by fifes, bassoons, and saxophones. Maybe it isn't laughter at all but a song they're singing, a smug, sneering, sinister song, lots of s's, a hymn of dragon triumph. No question: they're rubbing my nose in this god-awful botch of an adventure. But it turns out that they don't have the last laugh after all.

(Did Mr. McGulvey have a hand in this somehow?)

(Will hands haunt me from now on?)

Because: to the music-laughter of the dragons is added a laughter even worse. A note even more evil. A sourness even sourer.

A chill to end all chills climbs up my spine: yes, it's the psi-fiend, who's finally made it to the heart of town.

Discovering a species even more we-weak than Homo sapiens.

More we-weak than we, because individuality and individualism in any form are alien to dragonkind. Dragons are team players through and through. Always of one mind, one color, one poison.

But the battle royal is disappointingly undramatic. It's

over, in fact, before it begins. The psi-fiend enters stage left, looking like a perfectly ordinary person who happens to be wearing a cape. And there's a medallion on his/its chest, a sad reminder of Sergeant Sherm—as is, for that matter, the whole body, which is my body, or an exact duplicate of it. I shudder.

The dragons have no idea what they're up against. Even if they did, it wouldn't help them. The psi-fiend laughs, then makes like an ectoplasmic Hoover. A single ffipp that no one hears, not even I; the ffipp is in the subether, on another plane.

A blur in the air, a moment of disorientation, then the dragons, spiritless, drop like stones: by sheer coincidence, one into each window of the fallen, horizontal office building. The odds against this—one dragon per window—are probably three billion to one. It detracts from the realism of the scene.

I don't care, I'm glad the story's finished. All I want to do is go home and take a hot shower.

The only loose thread in the narrative now is the psi-fiend, since the dragons all got their comeuppance and Sir Josh and Sir Mike have been avenged. So what do I do with the psi-fiend? It turns to look at me, satisfaction on its face. It burps.

Looking at the psi-fiend is like looking in a mirror and seeing a face you can't deny is yours, even though it disgusts you beyond words.

The burp tells me that the monster has been neutralized. Neutralized, as in acids and bases. The egocentric/anarchic evil of the psi-fiend and the collectivist/coordinated evil of the dragons of Cuspidor have canceled each other out, the evils being equal and opposite.

I get a better grip on my loving cup and start walking to the bus terminal, which is only four blocks away.

The next bus to Pittsburgh leaves in an hour and a half. I sit in the cafeteria there and eat a bowl of chili while outside the sirens wail and wail and the ambulances and fire trucks race past, lights flashing, all in the same direction. I wonder how many people I killed, all told. There were probably a few hundred in the office building alone. More than a thousand on the ground. I think: I could murder someone right now, with my sword, or go to the ladies' room and rape a nun on the toilet, stuffing paper towels in her mouth to keep her from screaming, and that would be a mere drop in the bucket compared to what I perpetrated at noon today. And yet I don't feel like a criminal. Did the Nazis feel like criminals, afterward? I feel dirty, that's all. I know I'll never be allowed back into McGulveyland, because this dirt isn't the kind that comes off with soap and water. It's Cain dirt, permanent. So I'll have to find some hobby now to fill the hours not taken up by school, homework, and chores. A friend would help. I should have a friend. With a friend you can get through the day with a lot less effort.

16

On Monday, Sherman tried making a friend out of Fred French, three f's, inviting him over after school, but Fred was ill at ease in Sherman's small room, and after about half an hour they ran out of jokes. Priscilla the Pill, in the hall, as Fred left, gave Sherman a wide-eyed look, as if Sherman had swallowed a whole bag of marbles on a dare. What was so wrong with Fred? Sherman wondered. When he asked Priscilla the Pill, her eyes got wide again. You don't know? It was in the papers. Where have you been?

The Frenches, incest, Fred's sister, sexual abuse, Mr. French arrested.

Priscilla the Pill said "incest" like it was any other word, and then "sodomized" the same way, without lowering her voice or hesitating even a little. Without stumbling over the *s*. Perhaps, Sherman thought, she didn't know what "incest" and "sodomized" really meant. With a sick feeling in his stomach, he got out the vacuum cleaner and spent an hour cleaning and straightening his room, as if somehow Fred had contaminated the place just by sitting on the bed and breathing the air. Mom, discovering the cleanliness of Sherman's room that evening, made a big deal of it and said she was delighted, thrilled, he was turning over a new leaf, growing up at last.

On Tuesday, at school, Susan invited him over, but he refused, saying he had some chores to do. She called him Wednesday evening on the phone and talked to him for almost an hour, but he kept saying he had homework, even though it was obvious to both of them that that was an excuse, and they were breaking up.

Thursday, Sherman took two finals, and when he got home, he had to clean up the mess Terhune had made in the dining room, under the table, a pool of yellow-white vomit with little brown and red pieces in it. The smell was horrible. He shampooed the rug and took Terhune to the vet—on foot, since Mr. Pliscou was only four blocks away and always available, if you didn't mind waiting. It was seven when Sherman got back, and Priscilla the Pill made a big fuss about dinner not being ready. While she was yelling insults at him, Mom came home, looking more drawn and dried up than usual. Sherman explained about Terhune. The house smelled so vile, they couldn't eat at home anyway. Mom took them out for pizza, cursing at the car, because the fuel injection still wasn't working right. The mechanic, she said, was incompetent. The car rattled at lights and stop signs, and sometimes it conked out altogether. Every time it conked out, Mom said, "Shit." Mom said they should get rid of the car, but she couldn't afford a new one right now, though that, who knows, could change in the near future.

Sherman's pizza was yellow-white with little brown and red pieces in it, and it smelled like Terhune. Priscilla the Pill, too, only picked at hers, though she had claimed that she was starving. Mom yelled at them for wasting the food sitting on the plates in front of them. She also said that Terhune was twelve years old now, and it would be better for him and for all concerned if they put him to sleep. Putting old, sick dogs to sleep was something that people did. Sherman didn't tell her that Mr. Pliscou had said the exact same thing today. Terhune had a big tumor in his stomach, and it was only a matter of time.

17

Friday, after two more finals, on his way home he stopped at the drugstore to buy the carpet freshener they needed to get rid of the vomit smell before Saturday, when Mom's important visitor and probably future husband was coming. At the cash register, Sherman's eye fell on the rack of newspapers, and he almost passed out. There, between *The Wall Street Journal* and *The Philadelphia Inquirer* was, clear as day, *The Cuspidor Times*. Sherman bought a copy, wearing the matter-of-fact face of a juvenile delinquent buying cigarettes, as if he was a regular subscriber to *The Cuspidor Times*, though this was Penn Hills and not a half-baked adventure out of a magic library. As soon as he was around the corner, he opened the paper and looked for the body count. It took his breath away: twenty-five thousand. *That* many? He tried to visualize twenty-five thousand bodies lined up, side by side and head to foot, in rows and columns. He multiplied, a hundred, five hundred, a thousand. He saw corpses from horizon to horizon, corpses in all directions, corpses piled ten high and higher. The worst disaster in the history of Cuspidor, the paper said. Worse than the earthquake of '48, worse than the epidemic of '23 and the great train wreck of '59 put together, worse even than the meteor shower of 1882, which had coincided with the Fourth of July, when everyone was outside, on the rooftops, watching the parade. Sherman read on. The police had arrested the terrorist responsible, the one who had planted the dynamite, leaving fingerprints everywhere. Sherman looked at the photograph and saw his own face. It was George, of course, behind that rearranged furniture. They would put George on trial, sentence him, probably give him the electric chair, which meant Sherman was in the clear, off the hook—except that his face was on the front page of *The Cuspidor Times* for all to see. What to do? He was too young to grow a mustache. Sherman went back inside the drugstore and bought a pair of dollar-fifty sunglasses.

18

"Sherman? Please, take off those ridiculous sunglasses. I'd like you to meet John."

Mom is wearing so much makeup and jewelry, she's the one who looks ridiculous. She looks like she's planning on going door to door tonight trick-or-treating. And her perfume is overwhelming; she must have poured the whole damn bottle on herself. It's so obvious, and so pathetic. She feels desperate because her face is all wrinkles and she has a lot of gray hair now; if she doesn't succeed in nailing this poor John bastard tonight at supper, she'll never get another chance.

The name couldn't be more boring: John. Dishwater John. If he marries Mom, will he give me a hard time? Expect me to get a part-time job or to go to church on Sundays? Will he check my homework? Give me lectures on being mature? Insist I give up my last name? Insist that I call him Dad? Will he believe in smacking faces for back talk?

I have a sinking feeling like I'm in an elevator, even though chances are John will be a nonentity: just another person you have to wait for to use the bathroom in the morning.

John gets up from the armchair. I put out my hand to shake his hand. He's large, heavy. Then I focus on him and do a double take. Clean-shaven, no stubble. What happened to the stubble? In the first moment, that's what amazes me the most. All that bare skin. But, even clean-shaven, the face is a hobo face, and nothing in the world could disguise those gray eyes, amazingly clear, penetrating.

"You know each other?" Mom says, because my mouth is hanging open. She's surprised, too, very surprised.

I mumble something: We, er, we once went fishing together.

He shakes my hand—a big, warm hand—and smiles his slight, polite smile. I see little Billy LoBianco's hand flying through the air, fingers catching on the chain-link fence, and then the thought occurs to me that Mr. McGulvey has come all this way to punish me. To punish me for Billy, for the people of Cuspidor, for what I did to his library, for V. Snerk, who is probably six feet under now.

I deserve it, I deserve it. Tears well up in my eyes. I say that I'm ready to take my medicine and that I'm really and truly sorry, and that it's already the greatest punishment in the world for me to be banished forever from McGulveyland. But Mom doesn't hear any of this, I don't even hear it myself, the words are coming out like bleats, because I'm on the brink of bawling like a baby.

But Mr. McGulvey hears it all, hears every word. He nods, lifts his other hand, the hand not holding mine, and says: "Maureen, dear, could you give us a minute together, for man talk?"

Mom, of course, is only too happy to do that, and takes Priscilla the Pill with her. My sister looks back at me as if I came from Mars and had two heads—three heads—and then the door closes.

Mr. McGulvey points a finger at me, is going to say something, changes his mind, then pokes me gently in the shoulder, as if it's almost a joke or he's apologizing.

"You really shouldn't, anymore," he says.

I hang my head, nod.

"I'll be marrying your mother," he says.

How is this possible? He has a whole world to run. And he doesn't like women.

Yes, well, but he met Maureen, my mother, at a seminar on tax advising, and they hit it off, like old friends.

Tax advising?

It turns out that Mr. McGulvey is a tax man.

Then all those stories by Old Corduroy, about him not paying taxes, were hogwash. Just the opposite, in fact. But how can Mr. McGulvey like taxes, when he likes butterflies and potted plants?

They aren't mutually exclusive. Taxes, tax laws, accounting can be fun, if you go in for numbers. There's

nothing wrong with numbers. Numbers are restful, soothing. Numbers don't wilt or get black spots.

But—but he has a whole world to run.

Nonsense, he never ran it.

But all those people saying, "Get McGulvey," or, "Mr.
McGulvey will take care of that? . . ."

He was a maintenance man there, that's all. Now he's
returned to taxes. Being a maintenance man was a good
break, it provided balance. A man needs a change of
scenery sometimes, and a chance to work with his hands.

Mr. McGulvey—John—John McGulvey?—shows me the
tough skin on his hands, the palms, the pads of the fingers, and tells me that I'll have a lot more confidence in
myself once I learn how to make things, fix things. Refin-
ish furniture or do plumbing repairs.

Speaking of which, he leads me to the bathroom and
shows me how to adjust the float in the tank behind the
toilet seat. It's really simple: you just bend the rod a little
downward. "This'll stop that constant trickling sound from
the intake valve," he says. "Here, you do it." The trickling
sound never bothered me; in fact, I thought it was peaceful. Running water, babbling brook. But I bend the rod
the way he shows me, and, indeed, the sound stops, like a
whisper cut off.

"And," Mr. McGulvey says, "if the float goes bad, which
happens, and fills with water, there's nothing easier than
replacing it. You just screw it off. Counterclockwise."

He's about to show me that, too, but Mom calls, it's time
for supper, so we both wash our hands, dry them on the
same towel, and go down the hall to the dining room together.

In a way, I'm pleased with this development, but in
another way, well, no more adventures is going to be
rough, particularly with Terhune's death coming up. And
I feel bad—I guess I'll feel bad—for the rest of my life
about V.

ABOUT THE AUTHOR

MICHAEL KANDEL lives in the backwoods of Long Island, New York, and daily braves the Long Island Rail Road to work as an editor for a major hardcover publisher in Manhatthan. Two of his translations of Stanislaw Lem were nominated for a National Book Award. *Strange Invasion,* his first novel, was published by Bantam Spectra in September 1989. He is currently at work on his third novel, which deals—among other things—with the greenhouse effect and a man-eating lawn.

BANTAM SPECTRA SPECIAL EDITIONS

A program dedicated to masterful works of fantastic fiction by many of today's most visionary writers.

■

FULL SPECTRUM 2 edited by Lou Aronica, Shawna McCarthy, Amy Stout, and Patrick LoBrutto
NO ENEMY BUT TIME by Michael Bishop
UNICORN MOUNTAIN by Michael Bishop
STRANGE TOYS by Patricia Geary
RUMORS OF SPRING by Richard Grant
STRANGE INVASION by Michael Kandel
OUT ON BLUE SIX by Ian McDonald
THE NEXUS by Mike McQuay
THE CITY, NOT LONG AFTER by Pat Murphy
POINTS OF DEPARTURE by Pat Murphy
PHASES OF GRAVITY by Dan Simmons
GYPSIES by Robert Charles Wilson
A HIDDEN PLACE by Robert Charles Wilson
MEMORY WIRE by Robert Charles Wilson

■

On sale now wherever Bantam Spectra books are sold

DON'T MISS THEM!

*"He was born in fire, not knowing who
or what he was . . ."*

The First Book of the Kingdoms

THE WRATH OF ASHAR

by

Angus Wells

Born of fire, feeding on death, Taws, the powerful messenger of an evil god, rises out of the blaze of a world-spanning forest, sucking life from each man he encounters. His mission: to raise and unite the northern tribes in order to destroy the Kingdoms of the south.

Born of a simple noble and a former acolyte of Kyrie, an order of psychic healers, Prince Kedryn faces his first battle—in defense of the three kingdoms—with all the excitement of the kill. Little does he know that not only is he Taws' hunted prey, but Taws' prophesied destroyer as well. . . .

■

Now on sale wherever Bantam Spectra Books are sold

And coming in August
The Second Book of the Kingdoms

THE USURPER

DON'T MISS IT!